ROOFTOP

///

PAUL VOLPONI

speak
An Imprint of Penguin Group (USA) Inc.

SPEAK
Published by the Penguin Group
Penguin Group (USA) Inc., 345 Hudson Street, New York, New York 10014, U.S.A.
Penguin Group (Canada), 90 Eglinton Avenue East, Suite 700,
Toronto, Ontario, Canada M4P 2Y3 (a division of Pearson Penguin Canada Inc.)
Penguin Books Ltd, 80 Strand, London WC2R 0RL, England
Penguin Ireland, 25 St Stephen's Green, Dublin 2, Ireland (a division of Penguin Books Ltd)
Penguin Group (Australia), 250 Camberwell Road, Camberwell, Victoria 3124, Australia
(a division of Pearson Australia Group Pty Ltd)
Penguin Books India Pvt Ltd, 11 Community Centre,
Panchsheel Park, New Delhi - 110 017, India
Penguin Group (NZ), 67 Apollo Drive, Mairangi Bay, Auckland 1311, New Zealand
(a division of Pearson New Zealand Ltd)
Penguin Books (South Africa) (Pty) Ltd, 24 Sturdee Avenue,
Rosebank, Johannesburg 2196, South Africa

Registered Offices: Penguin Books Ltd, 80 Strand, London WC2R 0RL, England

First published in the United States of America by Viking,
a division of Penguin Young Readers Group, 2006
Published by Speak, an imprint of Penguin Group (USA) Inc., 2007

3 5 7 9 10 8 6 4 2

Text copyright © Paul Volponi, 2006
All rights reserved
THE LIBRARY OF CONGRESS CATALOGING-IN-PUBLICATION DATA IS AVAILABLE:
ISBN 0-670-06069-0(HC)
Set in Chaparral
Speak ISBN 978-0-14-240844-5
Printed in the United States of America

APR - - 2009

IT HAPPENED IN A MOMENT....

LIGHTNING BOLTS SHOT OUT OF THAT DOORWAY, and they didn't stop till the air all around us was on fire.

I heard the breath leave Addison's lungs, like he'd been slammed in the chest by a subway train. Then he didn't make another sound.

A bullet ripped past my face.

I jerked in two directions at once, diving to the floor. My arms crisscrossed my head, and my chin was jammed up against my knees.

"Police!" "Police!" voices barked, one over the other.

A voice I'd heard before hollered at us to stay down and drop our weapons.

My whole body was shaking, and everything inside me went numb.

A sharp knee jabbed me in the back. I felt the shock run up and down my spine. My arms got bent backwards, and the metal handcuffs cut into my wrists.

I wanted to tear them all to pieces for what they did to Addison. I could feel everything inside me boiling over, but there was no place for it to go. So I buried my face in the black tar and screamed out in pain.

OTHER BOOKS BY PAUL VOLPONI

Black and White

Rucker Park Setup

THIS NOVEL IS DEDICATED to examining the gap between truth and fiction—on all sides of the equation.

Thanks to my loving wife, April Volponi,
a diligent first reader.

Special thanks to editor Joy Peskin, Regina Hayes,
Rosemary Stimola, and Jim Cocoros
for their insight into this novel.

I would especially like to recognize the work of all the substance-abuse counselors who lent a voice to this text.

ROOFTOP

I **NEVER THOUGHT** I'd get so close to those teeth. I had a hundred nightmares about them since my parents pulled me out of Long Island City High School and put me in this drug program five months ago. Half the time, I'd walk the long way around just to not hear him growl at me, or feel myself jump when he threw his weight up against the chain-link fence. But even from the end of the block, I could see when his gate was left open. That's when I'd feel my mouth go bone-dry. I'd take one slow step at a time. Maybe he could smell me coming 'cause he wouldn't start barking till I was too close to jet back the other way. Sometimes he'd step out into the middle of the sidewalk in front of Daytop and stare me down. His eyes were sick and crazy. He'd pull back the corners of his mouth and show me his teeth. They were white as could be, and the two sharpest ones on either side came down beneath his lip. He was gray, with swirls of black and white mixed in. You could get hypnotized just trying to figure out where the colors started and stopped. He looked more like a wolf than a dog, and I never felt more like a piece of meat than when he was grilling me. But I wasn't about to let it go on another second. I couldn't live with myself if I did.

CHAPTER 1

THE DOOR TO Daytop would stick. So I turned the knob and rang the bell at the same time, pushing as hard as I could. My heart was pounding faster and faster, till I finally felt that door give. Then I shut it behind me just as quick.

"It's never locked after eight o'clock, Clay," said Andre, one of the counselors, who buzzed me in anyway. "You just have to push hard enough. That's all."

Andre always knew when that dog had me shook.

"All you have to do is stand up for yourself one time," he poked at me. "That mongrel's gonna keep on top of you till you do."

I held my breath and just nodded my head. Then I took off upstairs to the kitchen where Miss Della, the other counselor, was making breakfast.

I smelled eggs cooking from the bottom of the stairs. Then I reached the top and heard the tail end of a voice I knew from somewhere talking to Miss Della. I walked past the big freezer by the door and the counter where all the food was set up. He was sitting with his back to me, at a table full of kids. Right away, I recognized the way his shoulders stood out and the brown #32 jersey. My mind went sideways for a second trying to piece it all together. But before I saw his face, I knew it was my cousin Addison.

Addison was a year older than me, and he lived in the Ravenswood Houses, right across the street from the co-ops where I was. We hadn't hung around together since we were little kids. He used to be like my big brother—till our mothers went cold turkey on each other and stopped talking. And now I couldn't even remember the last time one of us was at the other's crib.

I'd see Addison on the street, but it wasn't the same. He'd started running with a crew of older kids, and everything we had got left behind. We hit high school and it was almost like we were strangers.

I knew he was dealing, and he knew that I smoked weed. But that was it between us. Then I didn't see him around for a while. The next thing I heard, he got kicked out of LIC and bagged by the cops for selling drugs.

But there was that spark inside of me when his eyes caught mine. I felt like I was ten years old again, and he was visiting my house on Christmas.

"Flesh and blood!" he called out, and jumped up to wrap his arms around me. "Miss Della, Clay and me are family," he said. "We're first cousins."

"We're all family here, Addison. This is your Daytop family now," she said, pushing the eggs from the frying pan onto a plate. "We're all trying to overcome the same addictions, and that includes your counselors."

"Miss Della, I'm not addicted to anything. I don't do drugs. The judge and my probation officer sent me here 'cause I got caught selling crack," Addison said. "I've been in programs like this before, and my urine always comes back clean."

"Do you drink?" she asked him.

Addison grinned, clasping his hands together out in front of him.

"Well, I'll drink a little something if I'm havin' a party with a proper female," he said, shifting his eyes to Ivy, the best-looking girl in Daytop.

"All right, then," Miss Della said, mashing her eggs down with a fork. "Alcohol is a drug. You'll learn that in *this* program."

Addison just turned away from her, rolling his eyes.

That's when Andre came upstairs, yelling at kids to lose their jewelry and do-rags.

"You should all know better. It comes off the second you hit the facility," Andre shouted. "Set the right example for our new family member."

"Fuckin' bling police!" somebody said under their breath.

But Andre just stared into the crowd of kids and let it go.

Addison popped the diamond studs out of his ears without a peep. Then we sat at a table by ourselves, and I clued him in on how everything at Daytop worked.

"Morning meeting's first. That's where we read the headlines and horoscopes out of the newspaper, and the counselors make announcements. Then they got a GED class that goes half the day.

After lunch, there's structure—we clean up the building 'cause that's supposed to show we care about where we are," I told him. "There's group session in the afternoon where kids talk about what's eatin' at them—stayin' clean, sex, their folks, all of that. And if you don't say somethin' yourself, the counselors will call on you. And if we piss 'em off, they can keep us an extra hour, all the way till four o'clock."

Addison didn't blink at any of that. He said it was better than jail, or the residential program he was in upstate. He asked me how quick the counselors were to call your PO if you screwed up. I told him kids beefed about it all the time, saying it was like the counselors had a gun to their heads.

"I never heard about you getting locked up," Addison said. "I know they're not exactly tight anymore, like back in the day, but I figure your moms would have said something to mine."

"It wasn't like that," I told him. "I never got arrested. I failed *all* my classes one semester and got caught at school with a bag of weed. Then the dean of discipline told my parents about Daytop."

"Yeah, I hate that bitch and her big mouth," Addison said.

"Well her daughter got a GED at Daytop and made it into college. That's all my parents had to hear, and they signed me into the program."

"Oh, shit! I'm mandated here, and you're mom-dated!" Addison laughed out loud.

It wasn't funny to *me*, but I laughed it up, too. And it just felt good to have something going with Addison again.

I gave him a rundown on the Daytop kids, and who flew what colors. But Addison shook his head and said there weren't any real gangbangers in programs.

"Kids here are just frontin' to look tough. I sell to all different crews. Hardcore cats couldn't mix like this without settin' it off every day," said Addison. "That's why brown's my color. It's neutral. I'm down with everybody, as long as their money's green."

Then Addison turned his head around quick to see if the counselors heard him.

"You gotta play like you're poor in these programs," he said. "If staff thinks you're in business, they'll lean on you over every little bullshit thing."

After breakfast, we went into the classroom where Andre ran morning meeting. Everybody stood in a circle to recite the philosophy. And Andre told Addison just to listen for the first few days, till he could get it all memorized.

"I'm here because I can no longer hide from who I am," everybody started together. "Until I accept that I am living a lie, I am running from myself. There is no safe haven for me until I can break the bonds of my silence. In fear, I am alone, lost to others as I am to myself. Only in this refuge is my true reflection visible. As part of a family, I can finally face that image. Neither lost in distortion nor draped in shadows, I can share my life and flourish. For in this new light, I will gather strength and grow, fearing not the solitude of death, but rejoicing in my love for others."

When I first got to Daytop, the philosophy was just words to me. But even before it started to mean something, it felt all right hearing everybody's voices together, saying the same thing at the same time.

"Cuz, that's a long-ass speech to learn," Addison whispered.

The classroom was regular-sized, with maybe twenty desks split up into four rows and a big round table at the back. There was a green chalkboard up front that shook for a minute whenever somebody wrote on it, and posters up on the wall with things like a skeleton saying, "Crack Is Whack."

Kids took their seats, and Andre started making announcements. Addison was halfway down into the chair next to me when he saw Ivy a row ahead of us. He moved up a space, and I followed.

Andre was saying how Reggie had stayed clean for three months now, and everybody clapped for her. Addison gave me a funny look, and then pushed his eyes towards Reggie. She kept her hair cut real close and always wore a long T-shirt. You had to look twice to see she was a girl and not a guy. Only she'd tell you right up front that she was gay. So I nodded to Addison to say he'd figured her right.

Latoya was rocking back and forth in her chair with her eyes closed, singing to herself. Andre stopped talking to look at her, and everybody was laughing. Latoya was real small. She was seventeen but looked like she was twelve. Andre had to walk over and tap her on the shoulder to stop. That's when Addison leaned over and asked me if she was a crack baby.

Bell was so stressed he couldn't sit anymore,

and he started walking around the room, jawing at Andre.

"You didn't mention my name about staying clean, so my urine had to be positive!" shouted Bell, his voice shaking.

"That's a private matter for staff to discuss with you later," Andre told him. "Unless you want to confess something to the family right now."

"This ain't my family!" Bell shot back, heading for the classroom door. "Fuck this program! I'm *not* signing any papers. My mother's *not* signing any papers. And I'm *not* going upstate to residential!"

Bell usually got his way with kids by getting loud. But he couldn't pull that thug routine with Andre, or bully his way out of a positive-urine.

I'd only come up dirty once since I'd been at Daytop. My friends were snapping on me one night, saying I was practically in handcuffs. I kept telling them how the program was nothing and how I could do whatever I wanted. So when somebody rolled up a fat blunt, I had to step to my words and get high. I drank cranberry juice mixed with white vinegar for two days straight, praying it would flush me out. It didn't. The counselors called my parents in for a family session, and they sat in Miss Della's office, looking at me like I was a junkie.

"You got to choose, Clay: your family or drugs," my mom said, wound up tight. "There's no room in between anymore."

"And that's no choice," said my dad, shaking his head.

"Lots of clients fall in the beginning. Now Clay's gonna have to watch every step he takes double," said Miss Della. "At least he's not in his old school anymore, surrounded all day by *those* kinds of friends."

At morning meeting, I had to tell kids how I fucked up. I thought that would be the easy part. But I really felt ashamed to say it out loud in front of them.

"I thought I was goin' good," I said. "Then I got caught out there tryin' to be somebody, and tripped up."

Andre gave Tony Soprano the newspaper and told him to read us the sports scores. His real name was Mario, but everybody called him Tony Soprano. He was Italian, and the only white kid at Daytop. Everybody figured for a white dude to get arrested he must have got nailed with a suitcase full of drugs and was probably down with the mob. Tony played the part perfect. He was into kids thinking he was "connected," and wouldn't say anything to put us off it.

Ivy got the paper next and read the horoscopes. I didn't even remember what month Addison was born in. But he raised his hand when Ivy called out "Gemini." His horoscope said that the twins inside of him were having a tug of war, and he should look to see which one got control. Then he would know what direction he was headed. Ivy knew I was a Leo, so she called out my name and started reading.

"Every sleeping lion awakes. Open your eyes. If the hills ahead of you look like mountains, take them one step at a time. Then you can build on everything behind you," Ivy read.

When she was through, Ivy handed the paper to Addison to do the weather. He read real slow, trying to make sure he knew the words before they came out of his mouth. But he got tripped up on lots of easy ones anyway.

"I haven't read out loud in the longest," Addison said, like an apology. "I definitely got to work on it."

I did current events. I called off the headlines, and if kids made noise like they wanted to hear the story, I'd read some of it. Then Reggie read a movie review. And when she was finished, she added her own part.

"How did this man get that job? I saw that movie. It sucked!" Reggie said. "It really sucked!"

Before Andre broke the meeting, he had Addison stand up and introduce himself to the family.

"My name's Addison Reynolds," he said, making his back straight. "I'm eighteen. I'm just here to do my time without giving anybody problems. I don't mess with people if they don't mess with me. That's all."

One by one, we told him our names and how old we were. Then Andre asked everyone to give Addison a round of applause.

"Tell him why we're clapping, Clay," Andre said.

"We're not clapping because you're here," I said. "We're clapping because you made it here, to a clean and sober environment."

Addison gave me a crooked smile, with his eyes opened wide.

"Thanks, cuz," he said, staring down at the empty desk in front of him, like I'd put a present there he never asked for and didn't want to open.

We started class, and everybody grabbed for their folders and practice books. I was working on the science and math sections of the GED. Except for those two parts, I had a good enough score on my predictor test to take the real GED soon. And if I passed that, I could get into a city college or get a job, or both. Then I could finish Daytop in a night group with adults, because I'd finally be one.

Andre gave Addison the placement test that shows your math and reading levels. He did the math part first, and it took him most of the morning. I even saw Addison counting up on his fingers a few times, but he kept at it till he finished.

In between parts, Addison took a break. Angel was sitting two seats away, drawing a lion out of a book on the jungle.

"So you get to draw pictures all day?" Addison asked him.

Angel didn't speak much English. His homeboy, Cruz, translated almost everything for him. And when we said the philosophy every morning, Angel just moved his mouth. Daytop didn't have any GED books in Spanish, so he mostly did drawings during class. Angel could copy any picture he wanted and make it look perfect. There was a drawing he did on the back wall of a kid hanging off the side of a big building with one hand. I told Cruz to let him know how much I liked it, but that he should have put giant springs on the kid's feet for when he fell. Angel used his arms and legs to show me the kid wasn't falling. He was climbing to the top.

Cruz stepped in, telling Angel what Addison had asked him.

But Angel pointed to the lion and then to me.

"This—for Clay," Angel told Addison. "Next one—you."

Cruz just smiled, like he did *his* part right. He started to tell Angel again, but Addison stopped him.

"*Amigo*," Addison said, reaching out a fist for Angel to give him a pound.

And the two of them connected on it.

On the reading section, Addison got stuck on the first story. I watched him read it over and over, before he even looked at any of the questions.

Bell was still bitching. He came back from a meeting with Miss Della, making noise. Addison shot him a hard look, and Bell shut his mouth in the middle of a sentence.

"My bad," said Bell, opening his folder. "I didn't see you was takin' a test."

Addison had only been at Daytop for a couple of hours. But he was already looking like top dog.

Class was almost over, and Addison had only a couple of the reading answers filled in. I could see him getting tired. His head tipped over to one side, and he almost nodded off. When the counselors finally called "lunch," Addison was the last one up. He shook his arms and legs out. Then he buried his test under some papers on Andre's desk, without ever writing his name on it.

For lunch, Miss Della had beef patties with rice waiting for us. Tony Soprano was the only one sitting without a plate in front of him.

"The white dude's being punished?" Addison asked me.

"It's that way every day with Tony," I answered. "He says Daytop food isn't worth the shit you take after eating it. So he doesn't."

You're not allowed to bring your own food inside the facility. Somebody could be sipping an orange juice loaded with vodka, or have a brownie baked with weed. Tony's father owned an Italian deli. And in the mornings, Tony would sit out front, wolfing down a hero from his father's store. Then he wouldn't eat a bite with us for the rest of the day.

Reggie ragged on him all the time about it, saying, "White boy thinks he's too good to eat with us." But most kids really believed Tony was down with the mob, and didn't want to mess with him.

After lunch, we had to do structure. Latoya had been at Daytop the longest—more than a year. But everybody treated her like a joke, so the counselors made Ivy the chief. She assigned kids different cleaning jobs and walked around with a clipboard, making sure everything got done right.

I mopped the floors upstairs, and Addison cleaned the classroom with Tony Soprano. I started in the kitchen, and by the time I made it into the hall, Ivy was standing at the door to the classroom. Tony was sitting down inside, watching with Ivy. The classroom was cleaner than I'd ever seen it. But Addison was still going strong. He was dusting all the books and standing them up on their sides, like it was a public library.

"That's how I am," Addison said. "A beautiful

woman gives me a job and I won't stop till she's satisfied."

Then Addison walked over and stood right in
front of Ivy.

"Do you like my work, chief?" Addison asked.

Ivy was hard to figure. Sometimes she wouldn't
even look at kids. She was already on a head-trip,
thinking everybody wanted to sleep with her. And
she was probably right. She'd stand up during group
and tell how she used to get drunk every night and
wake up with a different guy on top of her. Bell tried
the hardest to get with her. But she wouldn't budge
for him. So now he just called her a "ho."

I thought I might have a chance with Ivy,
because she always looked straight at me whenever
I said something in group. But I never had the guts
to move on it.

"The classroom's yours every day now," Ivy said,
walking away.

The three of us watched her ass swing from side
to side.

When she got out of earshot, Addison grabbed
the mop halfway up the handle.

"Give me some time and I'll be slidin' up into

that chick," Addison said, jabbing the stick into the air.

During group, Addison didn't say two words, and only opened his mouth to push back a yawn. Sometimes it looked like he was really listening to what kids said. But once or twice, his eyes almost shut.

"I'll let it slide today because you're new," Miss Della told him after group. "But you're gonna have to participate, or else you won't complete this program."

"Addison, what time do you go to bed at night?" Andre asked.

I could see the wheels spinning inside Addison's brain. But then he just gave up and said, "Earlier. I'll go to bed earlier from now on."

After he walked away, Addison said, "Yeah, right. Maybe they can tuck me in every night, too."

The second we got outside of Daytop, Addison lit up a cigarette. He had a brand-new pack, and he even let Angel and Cruz bum one. I was surprised when he tossed a stove Bell's way, too. I quit on cigarettes when I stopped smoking weed. But all that smoke had me fiending for one bad.

Addison put the diamond studs back in his ears,

and the two of us started down the block. The gate to the tire shop was closed, with the chain wrapped around it. I was on the outside of Addison when that bastard dog hit the fence.

Woof-woof, woof, woof, woof-woof!

My heart nearly popped out of my chest. Everything inside me sped up superfast, but I was too scared to run, and my feet just dug into the sidewalk.

Addison barked right back at him, and never stopped walking. And he and the dog kept at it till the dog ran out of yard.

"That dog thinks he's all that, but he's not," Addison said, looking back at me.

After another block, my breathing slowed back down to normal. The feeling came back into my toes, and I looked at Addison like he could walk through a brick wall if he wanted.

We passed Rainey Park and turned off Vernon Boulevard towards 21st Street. The Ravenswood Houses have more than thirty buildings, and we were just coming up on one end of them. When projects get that big, there are always parts where you're a total stranger. So you keep your eyes sharp to everything around you.

I used to live in building #16, the same as Addison. Then my family moved to the co-ops across the street. Addison's father is my mother's only brother, and he used to be a real player. But he had more than just a shorty on the side. He had a whole other family with two kids living in the far end of the projects. Then Addison's mother ran into them all together, and the shit hit the fan. Now he lives with that other woman. But I wasn't sure in which building.

"You're his sister, and I'm supposed to believe you didn't know he was playin' me that way!" Addison's mother barked on mine. "Don't pretend to be my friend, 'cause I know you're more his family!"

I remember my mother swearing to God that she didn't know. But Addison's mother didn't believe her. That's when everything got tore down between them, and Addison and me got cut off.

"So how does it feel to own the apartment you live in?" Addison asked. "Can you just tear down the walls or burn shit if you want to?"

"It doesn't work like that," I told him. "My dad says the bank owns more of it than he does."

We got closer to our part of the hood, and

Officer Henry was on the corner with two rookie cops. Henry had been patrolling the Ravenswood Houses since before I was born. He knew everybody by face. But if he knew your name, he'd probably locked you up before.

"You staying out of trouble, Addison?" he asked in a thick voice.

"I'm coming back from Daytop with my cousin, Clay," Addison answered, pulling his hands out of his pockets.

Officer Henry looked me up and down, like he was memorizing everything about me. He grew up in the projects, too, and knew every kind of game kids ran there. Henry was diesel and always wore short-sleeve shirts, so you'd see the muscles in his black arms bulging. Almost everybody I knew respected him and thought he was as fair as a cop could get.

The two white rookies were like toothpicks next to Henry. They didn't know whether to smile or try to look tough. The city sent newjacks to the projects to get an education, and kids usually had them turning in every direction.

"Addison's got himself a little problem standing on street corners," Henry told the rookies. "For some reason people keep walking up to him, tryin' to buy crack."

The two of them laughed with their heads bobbing up and down like puppets.

Henry's radio went off, so we started walking again. Addison raised his eyes to me, like we were a hundred times smarter than the cops. But all the way home I was thinking—Now Officer Henry knows my name, too.

CHAPTER 2

MY PARENTS WERE happy as anything that Addison was at Daytop. They'd seen him playing the corner and knew he was selling. Soon as I told my mom, she buried any beef she had and was on the phone with Addison's mother.

"You can't blame yourself. Damn my brother! Boys without a father in the house try to be men faster than they know how," Mom told her. "And that means making money on the street or getting girls pregnant."

Addison has a brother, Darrel, who's a year younger than me. He's into shit on the streets, too. But he's still going to LIC and doing enough to pass his classes. Addison's mother works for the police department. She's an operator and takes 911 calls.

She doesn't have a badge or a gun, just an ID card.

When I was little, she'd say, "Go ahead, Clay. Mess up and I'll send the police after you."

And I was always afraid of touching stuff in her house, thinking if I broke something she could put me in jail.

I don't have any brothers or sisters. So when our mothers stopped talking, it was like losing a big brother and little brother in one shot. That was right before we moved into the co-ops. I didn't know moving across the street could be like going to another country. Other black families lived in the co-ops—Spanish ones, too. But *I* was the new-jack there, and it took me a long time to figure out where to put my feet down.

I started smoking weed when I was fifteen. I couldn't tell you exactly why, except that it made me feel good—like my head was over the clouds. By then, Addison was already dealing, and a couple of times my friends and me copped weed off him. I'd brag that he was my cousin, and Addison would say how he ran his end of the corner.

"I got the smoke to make King Kong choke," Addison would riff. "Get you so high, think you can fly. Even the cops breathe deep when they roll by. That's no joke. That's no lie."

After a while, hanging out with my friends meant getting high. Then I started to like weed too much, and got blazed every day. I'd ditch school to smoke with my friends. There was more red ink on my report card than black. I even failed my best subject—English—because I didn't read any of the books. When my friends weren't around, I got high by myself. But instead of feeling good, I just felt more alone.

One night, a squad of supercops wearing bullet-proof vests rolled from the back of a black van. They grabbed everyone at our end of the block and had maybe twenty people with their hands up against the wall. Everybody calls them "TNT" because they make sweeps on Tuesdays and Thursdays. They didn't give a damn that it was Saturday. I looked over my shoulder, and a cop had his hammer out of the holster, pointing right at me. I was shaking all over, thinking I'd get shot.

"Do you have any weapons or needles in your pockets I could stick myself on?" snarled a cop wearing rubber gloves.

I was so scared I couldn't get a word out. So I just shook my head.

I didn't even remember that I didn't have any weed on me.

When that cop didn't find anything, he let me go.

But I got nailed at school with weed, and my dad took it personal.

"I bust my ass every goddamn day to get you a head start, and you're just pissin' it away," he went off on me in the dean's office. "Why don't I pull some kid off the street with nothin' and give *him* your room?"

He called me "weak" and a "loser" and said I'd be shoveling other people's shit my whole life. Mom screamed at him for that, and made sure to say how he used to get high at my age.

"Don't forget! You only stopped after the cops kicked the door down to your mother's apartment with their guns out and dragged your brother off in handcuffs," she snapped at him in front of the dean.

Then she didn't talk to either one of us for two days.

After his brother got locked up for dealing, my dad took his place driving a laundry truck. Now

Dad owns the whole route, and three more trucks. Addison's father is one of his drivers.

- - - - -

Addison made the first week at Daytop, and everything was straight. He was still doing business on the street, but he played along enough to keep the counselors and his PO off his ass. It was that way with most kids when they first got to Daytop. They only did the program because some judge was going to send their ass to jail if they didn't.

Then Addison missed a day without calling. Miss Della dialed up his house, and Addison's mother said he didn't come home the night before. Mom talked to her, too. His mother was worried sick because even Darrel didn't know where he was.

The next morning, Addison was waiting for me on the block before Daytop.

"Cuz, you'll never believe what happened," said Addison, limping as he walked. "My girl stabbed me on my thigh with a kitchen knife. I spent all day yesterday at the police station, getting everything straightened out."

Addison said he was at his girl's crib when she went into the shower. So he used her phone to call another shorty. Then he went out into the hallway to smoke a cigarette. When he went back inside, his girl had already hit the redial and knew how he played her. She went wild over it and stabbed him.

"Her mother, brother, and his girl were there, too. That's why I had to go into the hallway to smoke," said Addison, checking out my reaction. "Then she calls the cops and says that I smacked her. But I hardly touched her. So I had to say that she stuck me with the knife. It took a whole day, but we both made a deal to drop all the charges."

All the time, we were getting closer to the tire shop. I kept moving my head around till I saw for sure the gate was closed. Addison was waiting for me to say something, like his story was too crazy to believe. But I was watching out for that dog.

"Did the counselors call my PO?" Addison asked.

We came up on the fence, and everything was quiet.

He was stretched out inside his doghouse, like he was asleep. And only his front paws and the tip of his black nose were peeking out.

"I don't think so," I finally answered. "They called your house."

Reggie and Bell were coming in, too. Addison ran his story by them, changing it up just a little. In the kitchen, Addison told it to Cruz the same way. Then Cruz translated the story for Angel, and I got to hear how it sounded in Spanish.

At breakfast, Miss Della looked at Addison cross-eyed. He jumped straight into his story, but she cut him off cold.

"This isn't *Showtime at the Apollo*," she said. "We'll meet in private about it later, and maybe we can call your PO together."

Addison started rolling up his sweat pants to show her where he got stabbed. But Miss Della was already at the stove and wouldn't turn back around. Addison tried to play it off. But I could see in his face how worried he was.

Andre brought up a new kid for morning meeting. Addison and me recognized him right away. He lived in the Ravenswood Houses, and Bell knew him, too.

"It's my man Clorox!" yelled out Bell.

Everybody was laughing, except for Andre, who jumped down Bell's throat.

"What did you call him, Mr. Bell?" Andre roared.

"I called him Clorox, like everybody does. That's 'cause he looks like his mother put him in the washing machine with too much bleach," he said with a grin almost as wide as Clorox's.

Clorox was black. But there were streaks of white running down his face. You could see it on his arms and hands, too. I'd seen him in the summer with his shirt off, and he was that way all over.

"The young brother's name is Warren Martin," said Andre, with a serious look on his face. "That's how you'll address him from now on."

"Yo, Clorox, I didn't know your name was Warren," said Bell.

"Mr. Bell, you better check yourself!" Andre said.

"Why? You already shipping me off upstate. What else can you do to me?" asked Bell, with some real attitude.

Clorox is just a sophomore at LIC, and weighs next to nothing. But he already gets mad respect on the street from older guys. He'd been selling and getting high since I could remember. And he'd do almost anything to prove he was somebody.

Last summer, everybody was talking about how kids in New Jersey were Jiffy-Popping cops to get into some gang. So Clorox swiped the keys to his aunt's car. He didn't really know how to drive, so he just sat behind the wheel, waiting for the cops to make their rounds. When they turned the corner in between buildings, Clorox hit the gas and rammed their black and white, head on.

The airbags in the cops' car shot out. The two of them looked like they had their faces buried in giant-sized bags of Jiffy-Pop Popcorn. Clorox hit his head on the steering wheel and got a lump over his eye the size of an egg. He didn't try to run or anything. He stayed right there, so everyone would know who did it. After the cops cuffed him, Clorox was mugging for the crowd, and everybody was calling out his name. He was too young to go to Rikers Island. So they hauled his ass off to Spofford, the juvenile lockup, where he probably thugged every other kid out of their chocolate pudding.

Clorox looked right past Bell to Ivy and said, "You got it goin' on, shorty. You gonna bless me with those digits?"

"I'll smack the white right off you, little boy!" Ivy told him.

That's when Andre marched Clorox back outside,

and Miss Della came in to finish up the meeting.

"Clay, I could use a kid like that around here," Addison said low. "He'll fuck up so bad, it'll take *all* the heat off me."

— — — — —

Daytop has its own holiday called Guadenzia, and it was coming up inside of the next two weeks. Guadenzia was a horse that fell and broke his leg in the middle of a race. But he didn't quit. He got back up and made it to the finish line. We were all supposed to be like that horse. Drugs and alcohol broke us down. But we could get up and keep going, if we wanted to bad enough.

"Oh my God! We're supposed to believe a horse could run with a broken leg?" asked Reggie.

"Don't get caught up in the negativity," Miss Della said. "It's just a symbol."

Then Miss Della asked Latoya to tell us about the celebration, because she was in the program for Guadenzia last year.

"You come back at eight o'clock at night with your family. But you still got to show up early the next morning," Latoya said fast, like it was a race.

"It's a party, with food. Better food than they give us now. The counselors make speeches. And if you don't come, they call your PO."

Kids complained about coming back at night. But Miss Della said it was part of our treatment.

"I don't want to hear it," said Miss Della. "You do things in this program you'd never do on your own. That lets you see yourself in a new way, and you might become a different person."

That whole week during our spare time, the counselors had us making decorations and writing out invitations.

In between licking envelopes, Addison asked Andre, "So did you ever grade that placement test I took?"

"You didn't really finish it, so I can't give you a valid score," Andre sidestepped him. "Let's just say it points to a pre-GED level, and there are some skills we need to work on."

Andre gave him a book for fourth-graders, and Addison was pissed. It had a picture on the front of a boy playing fetch with his dog. And Addison read it with the cover pushed down flat against his desk, so other kids wouldn't see.

"This is why I hate school—teachers treat me like I can't tie my own shoes. Sometimes I wanna say, 'See, no Velcro! I got laces, assholes!'" Addison told me on the side. "On the street, if you're still in business, you got brains. And when you're makin' real money, you're 'The Man.' It don't matter 'bout your test scores. But I got to stress over my PO. So now I got to be the oldest fourth-grader in New York City, and probably the only one with a felony conviction."

Most days, for the first fifteen or twenty minutes, Addison was headfirst into his lessons. He'd try real hard, and I'd help him. Then his eyes would get glassy and he'd start to fade. He'd either fall asleep or get into some kind of trouble. Addison was always in special-ed, growing up. Only nobody could mention it in front of him, unless they wanted to get pounded—not even me.

The counselors never talked to Addison about disappearing. But his first day back, after group, they gave him a "haircut." That's where you face your peers and have to take everything they say, without arguing back.

Miss Della chose a crew, and Addison sat in a

chair facing Reggie, Ivy, Tony Soprano, and me.

"Family, what do you have to say to Addison about his actions?" asked Miss Della.

Tony and me didn't want to say anything too bad. But the girls couldn't wait to unload on Addison.

"First, you're not supposed to miss a day of program, unless you have a doctor's note," Reggie said.

"And if your girl really stabbed you, then you shouldn't go near her again," said Ivy. "Men can get stuck in abusive relationships, too."

Addison nodded his head and was trying to keep a serious look on his face. But I could see him fighting back a smile at how easy he was getting off.

Then Reggie and Ivy both said that his girl was probably high.

"How about something from the boys?" Miss Della said. "Remember, you're not helping Addison by staying quiet."

"You should have called in, so the counselors would know where you were," Tony said.

"That's right!" the girls said over each other.

"And if you don't call, it's because *you* know you're in the wrong place," I said, wanting to pull the words back the second they came out.

Addison stared at me like I'd sucker punched him when he wasn't looking. But part of me said it wasn't a joke, and I was worried about him.

On the way home, Addison wasn't saying much. He should have been celebrating over the counselors not calling his PO. But he wasn't.

I saw two women in short skirts and stockings sitting on a bench just inside the gate at Rainey Park. And I tapped Addison, so he wouldn't miss them.

"Damn, they're fine!" Addison said. "Let's check 'em out."

They were eating lunch and must have been twenty-five or thirty years old. One of them saw us coming and put her hand on her purse.

Addison made his voice sound extra mature and said, "Pardon me, ladies. But I was telling my associate that the two most beautiful things in this park aren't the birds and the trees."

They looked at each other for a second. Then one broke out laughing, slapping her hand against the bench. I stood there like a dunce, laughing with her. The other one thanked us for being "so sweet," and said they had to go back to work. Addison didn't miss a beat and told them we had to get back to our office soon, too.

It didn't matter that we got shot down. I was jealous of how Addison handled everything that came at him. He even showed that damn dog he was nobody to fool with. We had missed out on a lot of time because of our families, and fell into the same shit over drugs. Only Addison was in way deeper than me. But I felt like things would get better for both of us if we stuck together.

We stayed in the park and headed down the hill to the East River. There was a tanker as long as a football field steaming past. And at the edge of the water, the big smokestacks from the power plant were puffing away. I told Addison I must really be addicted to weed because they all reminded me of giant blunts.

That's when Addison told me his girl wasn't really the one who stabbed him.

"This posse I got beef with pushed me off my spot. Five of them jumped me for my stash and money. *Five* of them! They grabbed the knife out of my hand and stuck me in the leg with it. Then I came back and chucked a brick at them."

He told me how they chased him through the projects and had him cut off from our end of it. He couldn't even get home.

"I headed for my pop's building. It was maybe four o'clock in the morning when I knocked on the door. I heard his voice inside and saw an eye in the peephole. But he wouldn't answer," said Addison. "My own pop wouldn't come to the door for me! What did he think? That I was stoppin' by 'cause I couldn't sleep, or I needed help, big-time?"

Addison said he saw Officer Henry that morning. That he stood still so Henry wouldn't see him limping. He turned his pockets inside out, and showed him that he didn't have any drugs or money. And Henry even said that he was proud of him.

"I owe my supplier almost three hundred bucks. He doesn't give a damn that I got jumped for my shit," Addison said. "Now I got him breathing down my neck, too."

We walked back up past the baseball field. I remembered playing hardball there for the first time, with Addison and both our dads. The ball bounced up and smacked me hard in the lip. I was bleeding and started to cry. But Addison told me real baseball players weren't allowed to cry, because there were too many people watching in the stadium. Then Addison played catch with me for the rest of the day.

That night, I gave Addison my last fifteen dollars.

He said he'd pay me back, soon as he got in business again. But I didn't want any part of drug money and told him to keep it.

CHAPTER 3

DURING GROUP THE next day, Miss Della was discussing dealers. She said it took lots of smarts to sell drugs. That kids had to set up their money, do the measuring, and figure out how to dodge the cops.

"I don't know why kids don't aim those talents in better directions and really make something out of their lives, instead of dealing. I guess they're convinced there're no other opportunities out there," Miss Della said. "But it's not just about them. Do dealers ever think 'bout what they're doing to people's lives and families?"

Clorox said he wasn't a dealer, that he was a "street pharmacist." And that he didn't care about anybody but himself.

"It's all about the Benjamins," Clorox said, pulling a fat roll of bills from his front pocket.

"Those ain't Benjamins," Reggie snickered. "Those are fives and ones. For him, it's all about the Lincolns and Washingtons."

"They add up to Benjamins, dyke!" blasted Clorox.

Miss Della jumped in front of Reggie before she could slap him. Then Miss Della made the rest of the family set Clorox straight about the rules. How he couldn't use names to put other family members down or wave money around inside of Daytop, especially drug loot. Miss Della said if it happened again, we'd all stay till four o'clock. So kids grilled Clorox for real.

When the talk got back to dealers, Ivy said that Addison should be ashamed of himself for ever selling crack. Then Bell and Clorox piped in with big smiles on their faces.

"You a black devil, Ad," said Bell.

"Yeah, look what you do to your own peoples," Clorox crowed.

"First off, that was the old me, before I hit this program," Addison said, looking at Miss Della, who didn't move a muscle in her face. "Selling crack was just a job. If I didn't do it, somebody else was gonna. Why should other people make that money instead of me?"

Angel put his hands around his stomach and said something to Cruz. Then Cruz said to Addison, "He wants to know did you ever sell crack to a woman having a baby."

"Yo, that's one thing I swore I would never do," Addison said, shaking his head for Angel to see. "But no lie, I'd probably put my foot up the bitch's ass for asking."

"You got to," said Bell, looking around at the dudes. "Imagine if that was your seed she was getting addicted like that."

Then Ivy asked Addison if he would have sold crack to somebody in his own family.

"How about Clay?" Ivy pressed him. "He's your cousin. Would you have sold him rock?"

"Clay's a man. He makes his own decisions," Addison said, stumbling through the words. "Why don't you ask him if he woulda even come to me?"

"Because I asked you!" Ivy said flat-out.

"All right, no! I woulda never sold to Clay," said

Addison. "I'd have told him to keep away from the shit. That it was poison!"

"Then why didn't you treat the rest of your human family the same way? Just think about that, all of you," Miss Della ended it.

I was happy Addison wouldn't bury me in a hole that deep, even if Ivy had him under pressure to say so.

The next morning, Tony Soprano was feeding that dog from his hero on the steps outside of Daytop. I stopped short at the corner and watched him pull out a piece of meat from between the bread. He dangled it in the air, and the dog leaped sky-high, swallowing it in one bite.

"Cuz!" Addison said, coming up from behind me.

I almost jumped out of my skin.

He saw the sweat on my forehead and asked if I was having some kind of weed withdrawal. But I couldn't even answer. The dog took the last piece of meat from Tony's hand and disappeared into his yard.

Bell showed up with his suitcase. He was waiting on the Daytop van to take him upstate to residential.

"These Day-Flop counselors finally got what

they wanted," said Bell. "I swear, when I get off probation, I'm gonna stand right outside smoking a fat blunt just to fuck with them."

Bell said he could live without the weed. He was more worried about all the gang shit he'd heard went on there.

Everybody who'd been upstate to residential said it was rough. Kids there were uptight because it was their first time without getting high. They didn't have anything to do with their spare time, except fuck with newjacks who weren't down with any of the cliques. So they'd shoot five, bare-knuckles in the bathroom over anything, like what TV channel to watch.

"One-on-one, I don't care. I'll fight anybody. I'll take my lumps and give some back," said Bell. "It's that piling-on bullshit I don't like. I can't fight six dudes at one time. Nobody can."

"I've been there. You can handle it," Addison told him. "Just watch your back till you see how everything goes down."

Bell pulled up his pant leg and showed us the bullet hole in his calf.

"See this! Two dudes got into a beef at the weed spot last year. They pulled out gats and just started buckin'. I got hit in the crossfire," said Bell. "I know it's just the leg. But you get shot, and right away you think you're gonna die."

He said first the bullet felt cold inside him, like ice. Then the pain and fire hit him all at once.

"If you didn't shit yourself when you took that cap, you'll hold ground upstate," Addison said. "I guarantee it!"

"You know you're right, Ad," Bell said. "For real—I ain't nobody's chump."

I couldn't believe how Addison turned Bell's confidence around like that.

At morning meeting, Andre was all over Addison for not memorizing the philosophy. He could only get out the first two lines by himself. Then Andre stuck it to him good by having Angel try it. Without really knowing English, Angel got just as far as Addison did.

"In two weeks," said Addison, looking embarrassed. "I'll do the whole philosophy myself. Word to mother!"

Andre jumped on that train quick. He told kids it was their job to help another family member reach his goal—that if Addison failed, we all failed. So we should practice with him and make sure he'd be ready. Addison smiled and gave Ivy a look like she should be his study-buddy. But she just stayed blank on him.

Tony Soprano brought in a game called Ghettopoly, and everybody was playing it during free time. It looked just like Monopoly. Only instead of the regular pieces and properties, it had stuff from the hood. You could move a forty-ounce beer, a gat, a basketball, or a leaf of weed around the board. It had places like Hernando's Chop Shop, Northside Liquor, and Ray Ray's Chicken and Ribs.

Latoya pulled a card that read, *"You got yo whole neighborhood addicted to crack. Collect fifty dollars from each playa."*

She showed Andre the card and he took a shit fit. He called the game "garbage" and "racist." The box said that a guy from Taiwan who'd seen a bunch of rap videos on TV made up the game. And after Andre heard that, he hated it even more.

"He's making money off of our poverty," said Andre. "That's not right!"

But kids didn't pay any attention to that. They loved the game and wanted to know where Tony bought it so they could get one, too.

I asked Tony about him feeding that monster next door. He said his father always kept dogs like that around to guard the back of his deli, and that he was brought up on the right side of them.

"They mark their territory. You're either with them, or you're not," Tony said, locking down a whole corner of the game board to become a slumlord. "Trust me on this—they never bite the hand that feeds them. My father taught me that!"

Addison and Clorox borrowed the extra dice from the game and snuck into the hallway to shoot for money. We were making plenty of noise in the classroom. But underneath, I could hear their voices, and the dice hitting up against the wall. Addison sounded like he was doing all right. And by the time Andre called out their names, Addison was ahead forty dollars.

"It's chump change. But it puts me that much closer to payin' off my supplier," Addison said.

Guadenzia was in two days, and Angel finished his picture of the horse. It was so big he had to lay it over four desks pushed together to work on it. The horse was standing up on his back legs, breathing fire. He was painted brown and black, except for the red blood running down one of his front legs. And there was a look in the horse's eyes like nothing could ever stop him.

We hung the horse up over the inside door to the front of Daytop. It sent chills through me to look at. I didn't know how Angel could take an idea from his head and make it into something so real.

Angel kept backing up to look at it, till he was almost flat against the front door. I gave him a big thumbs-up. But he kept tilting his head in every direction to make sure the horse was straight. And when he decided it was perfect, he gave me a thumbs-up back.

The van picked up Bell right before the counselors took urines. Bell laughed all the way out the door and said, "Pee you later!"

A couple of times a week, our urines got sent out to a lab somewhere, and the report came back to Daytop. Only Andre didn't trust us alone in the bathroom anymore. He watched you pull out your dick and fill the cup, and Miss Della eyeballed the girls. When I first started the program, you could go into the stall alone and piss. But some kid was bringing in his little brother's pee in a bottle. Andre never even caught on that it wasn't warm. The kid got nailed when the bottle slipped out of his hand

and fell in the toilet. Andre walked in and found the kid with his arm halfway into the bowl trying to fish it out. That's when Andre became official dick inspector. He'd open the stall door and watch you fill the bottle, with other kids in the bathroom waiting their turn.

Sometimes it would get into my head. I'd have to go bad, but couldn't get started with him looking. I'd drink a gallon of water, and feel like my pipes were ready to burst, and it could still take five minutes before I got out a drop. Andre would snap at me about the time. Then I'd lock up tight and have to try again later.

"You just staring at it," Clorox told Andre. "That's homo!"

"Listen, I got one of my own and raised two sons. It's nothin' I haven't seen before," said Andre. "It's my job."

Clorox said he'd rather collect cans on the street than have a job like that.

"No thanks, I'll keep *this* one. I've had other jobs I wasn't so proud of. There was dealin', stealin'— even from my own kids—chasin' down anybody who owed me money . . . mostly so I could get high. And, oh yeah, bein' a full-time addict," said Andre, who came through the adult program at Daytop.

"Was you ever a pimp for Miss Della?" Clorox asked with a straight face.

Andre didn't answer him. And nobody else even cracked a smile, out of respect for Miss Della, who'd come through the program, too.

All through lunch and structure, Addison and Clorox were disappearing to play dice. Addison beat him for another ten bucks, and Clorox was hungry to get even. So after Daytop, Addison and me went with Clorox to his building where dudes rolled Cee-Lo in the basement, next to the laundry room.

There were three kids I recognized from the hood rolling dice on a Knock Hockey table on top of a broken dryer. They even had sticks and a wood puck to make it look innocent, in case the tenant patrol or cops showed up.

One of the kids was Addison's brother, Darrel. He gave me a pound and said my name over the noise from the washers and dryers next door.

"This a family game now?" Darrel asked his brother.

"I'm not playin'. I just come to pull for Addison," I told him.

"What, you got no love for my bankroll?" Darrel said, tapping his pocket.

It was hard to hear, so the shooter just held up his money, waiting for somebody to match him. Dudes on the side either backed the shooter or the kid going up against him.

Cee-Lo takes three dice to play. A 4–5–6 is a "Cee-Lo," and you win. Three of the same number is "trips," and you collect, too. A 1–2–3 is an "ace," and you lose. Besides those, the kid with the best combination wins. I didn't know all the rules, but I was figuring them out as guys played.

Addison was clicking from the start. He rolled a couple of Cee-Los and took the first few pots. He didn't lose more than two games in a row. And every time Addison doubled his bet, he won. After an hour, Addison had $140.

The dryers were throwing off hot air, and it was blazing in that room. Everybody was soaked in sweat, and the air got so thick I couldn't breathe. So I went outside to cool my lungs. And the second the door slammed shut behind me, all that noise disappeared from between my ears.

Little kids were laughing and screaming all over

the yard, playing on the jungle gym and swings. Some girls were jumping double Dutch in the corner, popping out rhymes with the steps.

"Miss Mary Mack—Mack—Mack,
All dressed in black—black—black . . ."

Twin girls were bouncing up and down inside the ropes with their ponytails flying. I knew their names were Celia and Maria. But I couldn't tell them apart. Everybody in the Ravenswood Houses knows their story. It was on the news and in all the papers. They were playing in the yard two summers back when their mother got shot. Two gangs were cranked up over something, and a stray bullet caught her in the temple. She died on the spot, right in front of them.

Anybody who saw it was too afraid to drop a dime on those thugs. And the cops couldn't pin it on anyone. So nobody had to pay in court. They just had to live with what they did on the inside. The same gangs run their colors past those girls every day. Some of the dudes probably even live in the same building as them.

Maybe the twins cry inside their house, when

nobody's there to see. But they don't stop for that out here. Their eyes are fixed on those scissor ropes, and their feet are a blur.

"She jumped so high—high—high,
She touched the sky—sky—sky . . ."

I went back inside, and Addison had lost some since I'd left. He was starting to risk more on each roll. Addison and Clorox split the next few pots. Then Clorox wanted to put up $100 at one shot, and Addison didn't back down.

Clorox rolled first, and threw a 2–2–5.

"Go on, beat that!" sneered Clorox.

The twos canceled each other out, so Addison had to beat the five, or roll a Cee-Lo or trips to win. The dice rattled inside Addison's right hand. And he shook them so hard the sweat flew off his wrist onto the table.

"I paid the cost to be the boss!" yelled Addison, letting them go.

It came out 4–4–6. Addison won!

But a huge black paw slapped the table, and the dice went flying. It was Officer Henry, with the two white rookies standing behind him.

"Don't anybody touch that damn money!" Henry screamed, stepping back to a metal box on the wall.

He pulled a fuse, and the sound of the washers and dryers died.

The nameplates under the rookies' badges read NEVIN and WATISICK. And their hands were glued to the guns in their holsters.

Henry pulled his summons book from his back pocket and said, "Illegal gambling. That's a seventy-five-dollar fine, unless you're on probation. Then maybe it costs you some jail time."

"Please, Officer Henry, gimme a break!" Addison cried. "The judge and my PO will flip on me. Please, sir!"

Clorox was on probation, too. But he kept his mouth shut and eyed the two rookies like they couldn't figure out how to put the cuffs on him.

Henry grinned and said, "I guess you are making some progress in that drug program, Addison. Maybe I should keep you there. Of course, your cousin Clay's in my sights all of a sudden."

Henry checked everybody's ID.

When he got to Darrel's, Henry said, "What a

surprise—another Reynolds boy. You gonna follow in your brother's footsteps, son?"

"No, sir," Darrel said, dropping his face.

Henry peeped Clorox and said, "Every cop in the precinct knows you, Jiffy-Pop."

"I'm a legend," Clorox said to the rookies, who cracked a smile for the first time.

Henry told everybody to pick up the money that was right in front of them and move over to the door.

"No, Mr. Henry. That's the money I just won," Addison pleaded, pointing at Clorox, who folded his pile in half and stuffed it into his pocket.

"I don't want to hear it!" Henry growled. "Now, one at a time, I want you to run across that yard as fast as you can. Do not pass Go! Do not collect two hundred dollars! Run straight home! Because if I see any of you on my beat again today, I'm gonna kick your ass a whole lot worse than this."

Then Henry kicked each one of us in the ass on our way out the door. I felt the sting from his boot on my behind all the way home. But I wasn't crying about it. Henry did Addison a real solid, letting us go like that. And now he was somebody in my book.

CHAPTER 4

THE NEXT MORNING, at Daytop, Clorox tried to
play like he never saw what came up on Addison's
roll. I didn't have to say anything about what I'd
seen. Addison took a fast step forward, cutting the
space down between them to next to nothing. He
was snorting flames, and Clorox's eyes were staring
straight into his jaw.

"You know I won that last pot! Where's my
money?" Addison barked on Clorox.

Latoya saw them from the kitchen and
screamed, "Fight! Fight!"

Before the counselors came, Clorox said, "I'm
just playin' with you, dog. You won! I'll have it for
you tomorrow. No sweat."

Addison already told his supplier he had the

money. But he backed off and said, "Tomorrow, that's all I'm gonna wait. Don't think you can play me 'cause we're in this program. I'll make you shit this place out your ass!"

Then they put a chummy look on their faces for the counselors, and Latoya caught an earful from Andre for crying wolf.

Clorox wanted to slap Henry for booting him in the ass. But Addison didn't care. He had nothing but props for Henry, and said the two rookies would have run us in just to spend a couple of hours in the precinct and out of the projects.

"You're just lookin' at doin' a bullet upstate. I'm facing three times that. If I blow probation, I'll do three years!" Addison told Clorox. "Those white cops would have sank their teeth into me for sure. I'm tellin' ya, Henry's all right!"

Everybody around our way hates the cops. All they ever do is bust on kids, and it's like we don't have any rights. Black and Spanish cops aren't any different. They mostly treat us the same way. But Henry's got something else going on. He talks to kids, even when he's slapping the cuffs on them. He tells them how they screwed up, and how maybe he made the same mistake when he was growing up in the projects.

I remembered watching Henry screw with a dealer one time.

"I know you think 'cause the drugs aren't on you that I can't do anything," Henry told some kid who kept his stash in a bag on the ground. "But I'm about to arrest you for littering. So pick that bag up and drop it in the garbage. Then you can say you got experience and apply for a summer job cleanin' the sidewalks."

Lots of cops would catch heat from the crowd when they locked somebody up. People would curse their ass out and scream how it was all a setup. But I never heard anybody disrespect Henry that way. I guess people figured if Henry arrested you, you probably deserved it.

No kid I knew wanted to be a cop. But Henry made you think twice, like you could be black and have that job, and not be a sellout.

During morning meeting, Miss Della went over what parents said they were bringing for Guadenzia the next night. My mom was making her macaroni and cheese. Addison's mood picked right up when he heard that. He used to shovel my mom's cooking into his mouth nonstop. His mother was making pork ribs in sweet sauce, and I remembered how crazy I was for them.

Tony Soprano's father was bringing a six-foot Italian hero from his deli. Cruz's mother was making some Spanish food I'd never heard of. But Angel was licking his lips and rubbing his stomach over it. The housemother from Reggie's group home was cooking collard greens, and Miss Della was baking buttermilk biscuits.

When kids heard that whole list of food, they started thinking that coming back at night wasn't such a bad deal.

Ivy and her mother were supposed to do a dance at Guadenzia. Reggie told Addison she'd seen Ivy's mother, and that she was a dime piece, too.

"So you don't just like other gay girls who look like guys?" Addison asked her.

"Hell no! One night we'll go out looking for bitches together," Reggie said. "Then you'll see what I like."

Kids always wanted to know how Reggie could live in a group home with straight girls and sleep in the same bedroom with them.

"Damn it! I'm a lesbian!" she'd say. "I'm not a rapist!"

There was a reading group at the back table with Addison, Clorox, and Latoya. Only they did as much ranking on each other as reading. The two of them were all over Latoya for ratting them out to the counselors that morning. So Latoya put her headphones on to cut them out and started rocking in her chair. That's when Addison and Clorox said they were embarrassed to be seen at the same table with her.

"No offense to anybody else," Addison said, "but it's like I'm in a retarded class inside a retarded class. I want to change my group."

"That's right! I'm in *special* special ed back here," said Clorox, looking right at Latoya.

Andre took Latoya's headphones away, and Addison and Clorox howled. Then he checked his grade book and said they both had a lower reading level than Latoya, so she should be the one complaining.

Kids cracked up over that, with Latoya laughing louder than anyone.

"Stupid is as stupid does!" said Latoya, over and over, till she swallowed wrong and almost choked.

On the way home, that dog was in the yard chewing on a big white bone. He growled at me when he saw my eyes on it. Then he got quiet, except for the sound of bone cracking between his teeth.

My parents were looking forward to Guadenzia. The last time they were at Daytop was because I fucked up and got high. Now it would be for a party. They still didn't trust me one hundred percent. But I knew the counselors would give them a good report.

"You don't realize it 'cause they're always pushing you so hard to do better. But those counselors are saving your life, Clay," Mom said that night at home. "Now I hope they can save your cousin's, too."

Addison's mother was coming over the next night, right before Guadenzia. She hadn't been to our apartment since we moved in, so it was going to be like a family reunion.

Since Addison started in the program, his father called our house more. My mom would take the phone into the next room every time. So I figured they had to be talking about us being at Daytop together, and that he cared something about Addison, or he wouldn't have been calling.

Clorox didn't show up at Daytop the next morning. Addison was kicking walls and talking like the kid screwed him good.

"He's thinking the longer he holds on to that money, the more he can flip it—buy drugs with it, sell 'em, and pay me off with the profits," said Addison. "But my supplier says if I don't pay in the next week, I'll owe him double. What if Clorox gets locked up, or ripped off? Where does that leave me?"

Addison even checked with the counselors, and they said Clorox didn't call in.

"I didn't know you were so concerned about the family members," said Miss Della with a straight face. "Are you treating Warren like a younger brother and looking after him, Addison?"

"No doubt, Miss Della," Addison said. "No doubt."

All day long, that dog was barking out of control. He'd slow down for a minute or two, and then he'd pick up again even stronger. Nobody could get any work done in class. Andre finally stuck his head out the window and screamed, "Shut up!" But nothing stopped that damn dog. I went to the window, too. He was on the sidewalk staring straight ahead at nothing with those sick eyes, barking like he was ready to rip somebody's heart out. And I was already sweating over getting past him to go home.

The counselors ended class early so we could put up the last of the decorations. Kids argued over what color streamers and balloons to use. Cruz did the whole hallway in the colors of his crew. Other kids wanted to pull that same trick in the different rooms. Then Miss Della got wise and put a stop to it. She even made Cruz go back and change the red streamers for orange ones.

Angel put up his last poster. It was shaded in pencil and divided right down the middle between light and dark. The outside of Daytop was on the light side, and a kid hawking drugs on the corner was in the dark part. Addison saw it, and right away he thought the kid on the corner looked like him. He didn't even bother getting Cruz to translate, and went straight to Angel.

"That's me!" Addison said, pointing to the face in the picture.

"No!" Angel said.

Addison kept saying yes, but Angel shook his head harder and harder.

Ivy told Addison that it was his conscience making the connection.

"You can't stand the truth about yourself. That's all," Ivy told him. "Why don't you admit it?"

If she couldn't turn up the heat by just looking at a guy, Addison would have sparked off on her for sure. But she opened her eyes wide at Addison and smiled. And he bit back everything he was about to say.

Latoya didn't have that kind of juice. And during structure, she was jawing with Addison over their reading levels.

"You be a good boy and I'll let you stay in my group. Then I'll show you how to read like a grown-up," Latoya said.

"Yeah, like a grown-up midget on crack, rockin' all the time," said Addison, holding his hands and arms in tight and out of joint.

During structure, Addison was cleaning the classroom and Latoya was emptying the garbage cans. Tony Soprano swore that Latoya threw the first cup of water at Addison from the cooler. Then Addison filled a balloon with water and dropped it on Latoya from the window when she took the garbage outside to the street.

Miss Della called them both into her office and put them on contract. They each had to sign a paper saying how they were supposed to act inside of Daytop. And that they'd be discharged if either one of them slipped up again over the next month.

"Children! Children! Children!" said Miss Della. "Sometimes all I think we have in this program are little children!"

That dog took one last barking fit, right in the middle of group. Andre was asking kids what it would take for them to go back to drugs and drinking. And everybody had to wait on that four-legged fuck to stop.

The second it got quiet, Tony said, "If I had the winning lottery ticket and lost it, that would get me back on coke."

"If I lost somebody in my family," Ivy said.

"After my mother died and I had no place to live, I got high every day," said Reggie, swinging her feet under the chair.

I couldn't imagine losing somebody that close to me and having nowhere to go on top of it. I'd be firing up every blunt I could find and living under a cloud of smoke.

Then Addison said it was like his father was already dead to him. But he wasn't going to blame him for drugs.

"That was *me* getting locked up. Nobody else," Addison said. "And my moms is a police operator. She coulda took the 911 call and been the one to send the cops after me. That's some spooky shit to think about."

That's when Cruz made the music from *The Twilight Zone.*

"*Du-du-du-du, du-du-du-du . . .*"

Even Addison laughed.

On the way out of Daytop, I opened the door an inch and peeked down the block. His gate was open, but I didn't see that dog anywhere. I hit the sidewalk and took off full speed in the opposite direction. Crossing the first corner, I almost got clipped by a car. Its horn nearly split my eardrums. But I wouldn't turn back around for anything, and I didn't slow down till I was halfway home.

At around six thirty that night, Addison and his mother rang our bell. I heard their voices over the intercom and buzzed them up. My whole family was waiting in the hall when the elevator door popped open. Our moms hugged each other around an aluminum tray that Addison's mother was balancing inside of one arm. And if Addison's mother was still holding a grudge against my mom, she had it hid to where it didn't show.

They came inside and my parents walked them through every room. Then Addison stopped to look out my bedroom window.

"You can see half the rooftops in the projects from up here," Addison said. "It's all right having a crib on the tenth floor. You know if it was me up here, I'd be spying down on some serious action, cuz."

My dad almost had to beg, but Addison's mother let us each have a pork rib before the party. I took my time with it, nibbling every last piece of meat. Five minutes later, we were all sucking on the bones. The taste of that sweet sauce lifted me up over everything. I didn't care that there was going to be a big tray of them at Guadenzia. I licked the fingers clean on both hands, so I wouldn't forget the taste. Addison was hunting around for my mother's macaroni and cheese, but that had to be heated up at Daytop.

"Why didn't Darrel come tonight?" Mom asked. "I haven't seen that child in the longest."

"He couldn't give up a night, not even to celebrate

at his brother's program," Addison's mother said, like she believed it. "He's got homework and too many friends."

Addison snuck me a look, like those were the last two things Darrel was busy with. But I already had that figured.

Kids were supposed to be at Daytop before the party to set up chairs and welcome everybody. So we kissed each other's moms good-bye and bounced.

In the elevator, Addison got quiet and ran his fingers down all the buttons. He had a tired look on his face that no amount of sleep was going to help. I thought he was going to say how his supplier or that gang of dealers had him under pressure.

"Clorox has got to come back to Daytop soon," I said. "He can't hide out forever. His PO will violate him."

But none of that was it.

"My little brother wants to sell crack," said Addison, taking a long breath. "I know the problems he's gonna get from it, too. I know everything that could blow up in his face. Even when things are good, a mountain of shit could fall on you any second from out of the sky. But after everything I did, and all that money he seen me count, how can I tell him not to do it? He's gonna look at me like, *Ad, you just want to keep that cheddar for yourself!* I can't do that!"

"You gotta make him hear," I said.

"He's not gonna listen. I know," Addison said.

"You can't let him go that way," I told Addison. "I'll be there when you tell him."

"The only thing Darrel wants to hear is how much money he can make," Addison said. "Look, I'm not sayin' I'd never sell again, cuz. But I don't want to see him take those kinds of hits."

The elevator hit bottom. We crossed the lobby and went out through the glass doors. It was almost dark outside, and the shadows from the Ravenswood Houses were running across the street. Everything Addison talked about was rolling through my brain. And I guess he was thinking on it, too, because neither of us said a word for the next block.

Clorox was hanging out in front of his building. I saw him first and turned to look at Addison just as he caught sight of him. Addison's eyes froze inside their sockets for a second. Then he jet past me. Addison had a ten-yard head start, but I was right on his tail. I don't know when Clorox saw us coming, but Addison made a quick turn, and the steps to Clorox's building came up fast. Addison's hand smacked the front door and I slipped through before it closed.

Their feet were rumbling on the stairs like a thunderstorm about to hit. I started up, too, and caught the back end of Addison turning the flight ahead of me. Then everything went quiet, except for the rumbling from my own two feet.

Addison was doubled over with his hands on his knees.

"That bastard either got off here or the next floor," Addison said between breaths.

We searched the third-floor hallway without a sign of him. But as soon as we reached the staircase, there were footsteps again, way at the top. We climbed up to the sixth floor, till only the stairs to the roof were left. Addison went up them on his tiptoes. He opened the door slow, stepping through. And I followed him.

The sun had just gone down. There was light from the moon and the windows across the way. We looked from one end of the roof to the other. Only there was nothing to see but blacktop.

Addison leaned up against the ledge and pounded it with his fist. Then he looked out at the buildings and lit up a stove.

"It's not right the shit that happens," he said. "It's not right."

We chilled for a minute, and I was hoping everything would pass. There were a couple of stars over our heads, pushing through the clouds. I was sucking in Addison's side-smoke, and almost asked him for one. The air was cool, but I could feel the heat pumping off the floor from cooking all day in the hot sun.

We stepped towards the door, and Addison thought he heard Clorox.

"That kid's gonna shit bricks over this!" said Addison.

Addison flicked his cigarette over the ledge, and I watched the spark of light disappear into the darkness. He took out his wallet and held it between his hands like a gun. It happened so fast, I didn't have a chance to tell him not to do it.

There were footsteps coming up the stairs, and

Addison crouched down by the door. When they stopped, Addison jumped up with the wallet pointing out in front of him and yelled, *"Bam! Ba—"*

Lightning bolts shot out of that doorway, and they didn't stop till the air all around us was on fire.

I heard the breath leave Addison's lungs, like he'd been slammed in the chest by a subway train. Then he didn't make another sound.

A bullet ripped past my face.

I jerked in two directions at once, diving to the floor. My arms crisscrossed my head, and my chin was jammed up against my knees.

"Police!" "Police!" voices barked, one over the other.

A voice I'd heard before hollered at us to stay down and drop our weapons.

My whole body was shaking, and everything inside me went numb.

A sharp knee jabbed me in the back. I felt the shock run up and down my spine. My arms got bent backwards, and the metal handcuffs cut into my wrists.

Someone was on the radio, calling for an ambulance.

"Rush the bus!" the voice howled. "Perp down! Rush the bus!"

I saw Henry's shadow giving Addison mouth to mouth. He had his hands on Addison's chest and was pumping with all his strength. And when Henry finally gave up, I felt my heart skip a beat.

There was a beam of light around Addison. His eyes were open, and he was looking straight up. I could see the blood covering his brown sweatshirt.

"Where is it?" the cops asked each other in a panic.

Then Henry cursed everybody's mother, and said it was a wallet.

One of the rookies ran his hands through my pockets.

I didn't want any of those bastards touching me. I wanted to tear them all to pieces for what they did to Addison. I could feel everything inside me boiling over, but there was no place for it to go. So I buried my face in the black tar and screamed out in pain.

A flashlight flooded my eyes.

"Where's the gun, kid?" one of them said, shaking me. "Talk! Where's the gun?"

A white hand grabbed me around the mouth, and I tried to bite down on it.

I could hear the sirens twisting towards us through the streets.

In minutes, more and more cops were on the roof. EMS workers were standing over Addison, but they weren't doing anything to help. There were radios going off and enough lights to make you believe it was daytime.

Somebody was holding my ID and calling me "Clayton," like he knew me.

Cops were filming us with video cameras from every angle. Only this wasn't a fucking movie. It was for real. And I already knew that Addison wasn't going to get up and walk away when it was over.

My mind couldn't focus on anything past that roof. Right then, there was nothing else in the world, except what was in front of me. No family. No friends. Nothing. There was nothing to grab on to and hold tight, and without Addison, all I had for sure was the rooftop underneath me.

The cops stood me up fast, with my hands still cuffed behind me, and everything started spinning. There was somebody standing on either side of me, holding me straight. And I thought I was going to throw up.

They took me past Addison. He was covered up with a white sheet.

At the doorway, I looked straight down the stairs and thought they were shoving me headfirst off a cliff. So I turned my feet into solid blocks. I looked back at Addison and cried out, "Flesh and blood! Flesh and blood!"

CHAPTER 5

DAD SAW ME from the hallway, through the glass window cut into the wall. He rushed into the room and past the detectives, like they were invisible. He wrapped his arms around me and wouldn't let go. Then my dad rocked me from side to side, and squeezed so hard he almost broke my back. I couldn't remember the last time he hugged me. I just knew that it was before I'd messed up with drugs.

"Thank God you're all right!" Dad said. "Thank God!"

My face was pressed into his shoulder, and I didn't want to see anything in front of me. I wanted to be a little kid again and have him carry me home. But I was too old for that.

From the second the cops took me off that rooftop, I felt a hole growing inside my chest. They took me just a couple of blocks to the police station built into the side of one of the project buildings. Everything around me was the same—the streetlights, the sidewalk, the sky—everything. Only Addison was missing.

I was going right back to where I was before, surrounded by my family. But there wasn't going to be any second chance for Addison. He was gone.

The detectives had been hounding me to talk. They never once sounded like we were on that roof to do anything but jack somebody or score drugs. I wouldn't tell them anything, except that Addison was my cousin, and my parents and his mother were at Daytop.

"My son doesn't want to hear any of your damn questions. He just watched a pack of animals with badges shoot his cousin, my nephew, to death," Dad said, fighting back tears. "We don't want to be here. Can't you understand that?"

That's when my mom's face jumped into my head. I knew if she wasn't there, she was with Addison's mother at the hospital or the city morgue. And somebody was going to pull back that white sheet to show them it was really him.

I wanted to cry more than anything. But I couldn't.

That hole inside me drained everything, and I couldn't find a single tear.

A black detective came in, talking in an easy voice.

"You're right. Maybe you should take your son home for now to get some rest. The questions we have are important, but we can ask them tomorrow when Clay's head's a little clearer," the detective said, rubbing the side of his face. "I understand the grief you're dealing with, Clay. And you have my sympathy. I know that in the morning you'll be able to give us the information we need."

On our way out the door, my father stopped and said, "Son, let me introduce you to Mr. Good Cop. He's the flip side of the twins, Good Cop/Bad Cop. And don't be fooled 'cause he's black. He ain't nothin' but a wolf dressed up in sheep's clothes."

We saw the crowd on 21st Street outside Clorox's building. There were cop cars everywhere, and TV trucks with satellite dishes on top.

Everybody in the street was talking about what happened. I heard the story piece by piece as my dad pulled me through the crowd.

"We're nothing but target practice for them!" "He

*was just a young boy!" "These trigger-happy bastards
don't give a shit!"*

None of them knew it was me on that roof, or
who Addison really was. I was just one of the faces
in the street, and Addison was another kid from
the projects who got gunned down by the cops.

We walked straight into a woman holding a
candle. She was old enough to be somebody's
grandmother, and there were people standing
around, listening to her talk.

"The TV said he didn't have a gun. That they
found a wallet in his hand. Sweet Jesus! A wallet!"
she said, stamping her foot on the concrete. "I'll tell
you why they shot him—'cause he was young and
black, and they could! That's why!"

I closed my eyes and could see Addison pointing
his wallet like a gun. And that hole in my chest
began to ache even worse.

My dad pushed me past them all.

That's when I saw the sharp teeth and pointed
ears. Every muscle inside of me pulled tight. I dug
my nails into my dad's arm, till he tried to jerk away.
A police dog was staring me in the face, panting
with his mouth half open. He was calm as could be,

like he wanted me to reach out my hand to pet him.

Dad couldn't budge me.

"Clay! Clay, what's wrong?" he hollered at me, frantic.

But I stayed frozen like that till the cop yanked on his leash and that dog disappeared into the crowd.

At home, my dad had the same questions for me as the cops.

"I want to hear it straight up, Clay. The two of you were supposed to be at Daytop. What were you doing on that roof?" Dad demanded.

I told him we were chasing some kid who owed Addison money, and my dad exploded.

"From drugs? He owed money from buying drugs!" he shouted.

"No! It wasn't like that!" I said. "Addison shot dice with this kid and—"

But I could see in his face there was no pushing him off that idea.

"Clay, it's all from drugs! Where do you think the money for that comes from?" he asked, without waiting for an answer. "You shoulda learned at least *that* by now!"

I turned away quick and headed for my room. I shoved open the door and walked into the dark. Then it hit me hard all at once, like walking face-first into a brick wall. Straight out my window, I could see the lights from two rooftops across. There were cops standing around, and I could see the spot marked off where Addison got killed.

I shut my eyes tight. But that scene was already burned into my brain.

Something inside me was screaming out—I wanted to get high more than anything. I wished I was stoned off my ass, so I wouldn't have to feel anything. I dropped to my knees and put my palms down into the carpet, gasping for every breath I could find. Then I crawled out of the room and couldn't go back inside.

I was asleep on the living-room couch when my dad woke me.

It was just light outside.

Dad was wearing a suit and tie and told me to get dressed proper, too.

I went into my room with my eyes down on the floor and closed the shades. Then I found the light switch and put on my good clothes.

There were two police cars parked outside Addison's building. The TV trucks from the night before were there, too, and a long black limo was parked on the grass. The cops eyeballed us up and down as my dad and me went inside.

We used to live on the third floor, down the hall from Addison. It had been almost seven years since I was in that building. I came off the elevator and saw our old front door. It had been painted over, but I could still see the dents Addison and me put in it, playing with a hardball. I wanted to stop and run my hand over every one of them, but my dad kept walking.

There was a guy in a black suit standing outside the door to Addison's apartment. He was diesel from the floor up. Dad told him who we were, and he let us past.

"Oh, my baby," Mom cried, hugging me.

She'd spent the night with Addison's mother, who I could see standing behind my mom. Her eyes caught mine, and I couldn't turn away. I wanted to say something, but I didn't know the words. My lips started to move, and Addison's mother said, "I know, child. I know." Then the tears started down her face. She put her arms around my mom and me, and in all my life, I never felt so warm and cold at the same time.

"This must be Clay," a sharp voice said from over my shoulder. "I'm Councilman Jackson Spiers. You have my deepest sympathy, young man, for your loss and what you've been through."

He reached his hand out to shake mine.

I'd seen Spiers on TV a thousand times talking about how black people got shitted on every day in New York City. He looked much older and smaller, standing in front of me. But when he shook my hand, his grip was like steel.

Besides the bone-crusher at the door, Spiers had two assistants with him. One was holding the remote, clicking through the TV channels. The other was on the phone, taking notes on a long yellow pad.

Spiers's hair was white as cotton. His teeth were huge and looked too big for his mouth. And every time Spiers talked, I kept staring at how white they were.

Darrel came in from outside. He walked up to me, and I could smell the weed on his breath.

"Clay, tell me how it happened," Darrel said. "I got to know now."

I told him how we were chasing Clorox, and Darrel blew a fuse.

"I'll kill that streaked-white motherfucker!" howled Darrel.

"Darrel, stop!" his mother screamed.

"No! That bastard got my brother shot dead over some chump change. Now I'm gonna chump *him* off!" Darrel said, heading back outside.

"No, you're not!" shouted his mother.

Dad wrestled Darrel into a bear hug, and the bone-crusher blocked the door.

"There isn't gonna be any more violence! You're not gonna kill anybody! I won't lose both my boys! You hear me, Darrel?" his mother screamed through her tears. "Do you hear?"

"You don't need to give your mother any more grief, son," Spiers told him. "The police are to blame here. They pointed the guns, not some other young brother trapped in these projects, too."

Darrel broke down bawling, and my dad took him into the bedroom. Then Spiers asked me to tell him what happened right before the shooting started.

I said how Addison popped into the doorway. I raised my arm out in front of me with my fist balled up tight, acting as the wallet. That's when Spiers's hand swallowed up my fist. He pulled my fingers apart and said, "Your cousin was trying to show them his ID inside the wallet. Wasn't he, Clay? Addison saw it was the police. He was scared, and he tried to show them his ID!"

I looked at Addison's mother. Pain covered every inch of her face, and my blood started to boil, thinking about how those cops blew Addison away. I wanted to strangle those white rookie bastards, and Henry, too.

Henry had the walk and talk down cold. But maybe he was no better than the rest of them. Maybe he was really another wolf in sheep's clothes.

Spiers didn't loosen his grip till I said, "Yeah, that's how it happened."

"And you didn't hear the police identify themselves before the shooting?" Spiers asked.

I shook my head—no.

I was turning circles inside that living room, and the sweat was pouring off me. I wanted to cry like Darrel. I wanted to be high, too, and kick the shit out of Clorox for getting us up on that roof. And I wanted to take back that lie I told about the wallet, but there was no way to do it.

One of Spiers's assistants found the police commissioner on TV, talking about the cops who killed Addison.

"From what I know so far, the shooting appears totally unjustified. I don't see any reason why these officers should have fired their weapons," the commissioner said.

"Damn right, there was no reason!" my mom shouted at the TV.

"He might have just thrown a real sucker punch," Spiers said. "He knows better than to say these cops are guilty before the investigation's finished. They'll get indicted, and their lawyers will say they can't find a fair jury. That the public heard the commissioner pronounce them guilty before the facts were in."

"It's all a game to them," Addison's mother said low.

Then Spiers's other assistant handed him the phone.

"Yes, Mr. Mayor. The family would be willing to

receive you this morning," said Spiers, nodding his head at Addison's mother, till she nodded back. "Of course, you want to pay your respects."

When he hung up, Spiers explained that the mayor was coming because he wanted to keep peace in the projects, and not lose votes from black people.

"I pray you win the next election," Mom told Spiers. "This city needs a black mayor again. Then these cops would have to think twice."

"Lord willing," Spiers said, looking up at the ceiling. "Lord willing."

I knew Spiers had run for mayor before. Posters of his face got pasted up all over the projects. And I'd seen stories in the paper about how he was going to run again. My old social studies teacher said that together, there are more black and Spanish people in New York City than whites. And if they all voted the same way—a white dude couldn't get elected dogcatcher.

Even after Spiers lost, those posters stayed up for months. And I remember seeing his face every day, till the rain and snow washed it almost pure white.

A half hour before the mayor came, Addison's

father showed up. Spiers talked Addison's mother into calling him and squashing their beef for now.

Addison's father looked torn up from the inside out. His eyes were red and nearly swollen shut, like he'd been crying nonstop for hours.

"Where's my son? Where's my other son?" he called out.

Darrel stepped out of the bedroom, and his father threw his arms around him. But Darrel played him off and broke loose as quick as he could.

I wanted to hate my uncle for turning his back on Addison and not answering the door that night he got chased all over the projects. But my mom held him tight, and that helped to soften me up.

Later, Addison's father looked me square in the eye and said, "I'm glad you're not hurt, Clay."

The mayor came with three assistants, and two of them were black.

Dad said one of them was probably there to translate Ebonics, and the other had to show the mayor's driver where the projects were.

Spiers sat on the couch between Addison's mother and father, and the mayor was in a stiff wooden chair, facing them. The mayor talked in a quiet voice and seemed sorry as he could be. He never mentioned Addison getting locked up for selling crack. But he knew about Daytop, and said how proud his family must have been that Addison was getting himself turned around. Then he said the officers would have to account for what they did. And if they didn't act inside the law, he'd make sure the DA pressed charges.

"Badges or not, they'll be treated like anybody else. I can promise you that!" the mayor said, raising his voice for the first time.

That's when Addison's mother let loose a sob. The mayor handed her the white handkerchief from the front pocket on his suit. He thanked her for doing her job, taking 911 calls, and said the city owed her something back.

If the mayor was playacting, he had it down perfect. And I couldn't tell. I just knew that Addison had to get killed by the cops before the mayor would ever show his face in the Ravenswood Houses.

Then the mayor went downstairs to talk in front of the TV cameras. He had his black assistants standing right behind him. But that didn't stop people outside from booing his ass. Spiers stood facing the crowd, way off to the side and out of the picture.

"It's a tragedy whenever a life is taken, especially one so young and just starting out," the mayor said. "I spoke with the parents and family members of the young man this morning and offered my deepest condolences. I want everyone to know that my office will do everything in its power to scrutinize the actions of the officers involved and protect the victim's rights. As you know, two of the officers are new to the force and in their probationary period. The other is a twenty-year veteran, and an African-American. Preliminary reports indicate that a total of four shots were fired, and all three officers discharged their weapons. I ask you all to be patient while we protect the process and let the investigation take its course."

Reporters dogged the mayor all the way to his car, firing off questions.

"Police Commissioner Lieber has already called the shooting 'unjustified.' What's your reaction to that?"

"Is it true that two of the officers were treated for trauma at an area hospital after the shooting?"

"The victim has a criminal record as a convicted drug dealer. Should that have any bearing here?"

The car door slammed shut, and the cops stopped traffic going both ways on 21st Street till the mayor was gone.

Spiers stood on the steps of Addison's building. His assistants brought Addison's mother and father down to stand next to him, and the reporters came running back, sniffing for more.

"Another cold-blooded killing of an unarmed black man. Are any of us really surprised? If you're young and black in this city, carrying your ID in a wallet can be hazardous to your life," said Spiers.

"Speak the truth, Brother Jackson. Speak the truth!" yelled out somebody in the crowd.

"The mayor wants us to be patient. At least Police Commissioner Lieber doesn't need a report for a backbone," Jackson started up again. "He's already called the shooting 'unjustified.' But that doesn't go far enough. We call it criminal! It's true, four shots isn't forty-one, like the number that killed our unarmed West African brother in the Bronx. And I suppose this administration would call that progress. But *one* bullet is too many. And that's all it took. We know from the doctors on duty that Addison Reynolds died from a single bullet wound to the chest. That could have been any of our sons last night. The mayor says that one of the officers was African-American, like he was throwing us a bone. Today the police will hear *our* witness, the cousin of the deceased, *who was on that rooftop*! Then we'll make our voices heard at the DA's office till he brings charges. And we'll find out if DA stands for 'district attorney' or 'damn accomplice.'"

Later on, at the police station, Spiers sat on one side of me and my dad on the other. I answered every question the cops had. And when I got to the part about Addison putting his wallet out in front of him, I could feel Spiers lean all his weight up against me.

"Addison had his wallet out in front of him," I said, clearing my throat. "He was reaching for his ID."

Then I pushed my toes into the floor, just to feel for something solid.

The cops asked me if Addison ever pretended like he had a gun.

"That's insane!" Spiers barked at them. "These

boys were committing no crime on that rooftop, and you want to know if Addison Reynolds aimed his wallet at three armed police officers. Please! We've had enough!"

Spiers stood up and walked us out. I stayed in tight behind him. But as soon as we got outside, I could feel the wind ripping through that hole in the middle of my chest.

At home, Mom said I was going back to Daytop the next morning. That she didn't want me staying home and having any more trouble find me.

Both Andre and Miss Della called.

"Your Daytop family has you in their prayers," Miss Della told me.

That family talk the counselors were always pushing touched me deep this time. Maybe because Addison and me got so much tighter there.

Andre said, point-blank, "You need to be back here. You'll want to feel better, and those drugs will be callin' your name. Don't answer them, Clay. Don't answer!"

Only I didn't tell him how loud I'd already heard them.

By nine o'clock that night, I was exhausted. I

just wanted to sleep and close my eyes to everything. I looked out the window in my room, thinking that rooftop would be dark. But there must
have been a hundred candles burning. And that
roof looked like it was on fire.

CHAPTER 6

IT STAYED DARK the next morning, and it was raining from the second I opened my eyes. On my way to Daytop, it started coming down in buckets. All around me, it sounded like a thousand hammers beating on concrete. And when a blast of wind turned my umbrella inside out, I ditched it.

The sidewalk was a sheet of water. It soaked through my sneakers, and every step I took got heavier. I was so cold and wet it didn't matter anymore, so I took the long way around and came up the far end of the block. That monster's gate was swung wide open. There was a river running down into the street off the little hill in his yard, and I kept wiping the water from my eyes, watching for him.

I didn't know if Clorox would be at Daytop, or

what I was going to do if he was. I wanted to get at him bad. But I was scared, too. I was scared I'd just sit there. That it would turn into one more thing eating at me, and that hole in my chest would just get bigger.

I walked in, and Angel's horse was staring back at me from over the inside door. I thought it would jump right off the wall and go charging down the street, broken leg and all. I passed underneath it and swallowed hard.

"I'm glad you're here," Andre said from behind the front desk. "This is gonna be a real test for all of us, but especially you. You're an inspiration to the family, Clay. It takes a lot of guts to tell *our* side of the story, 'cause the cops are gonna tell theirs different. So stay strong, my young brother."

Then he handed me a towel, and I dried my face.

All the way upstairs, I could hear the water squeezing out of my kicks.

The kitchen was dark. Breakfast was already made and laid out inside the classroom. Everybody's eyes jumped to me. But Miss Della told kids to stay in their seats and give me space to breathe.

I went through everybody's face twice to make sure—Clorox wasn't there.

"Bring breakfast back to your seat, Clay," said Miss Della. "We're doin' things a little different today—eating in the classroom. We can see each other better here. I know we've all got plenty to say about how we feel, but we're gonna keep it to ourselves till everybody's together."

I heard the door open behind me, and my heart stopped till I saw it was Latoya.

Nobody seemed like they really cared about eating. Only Tony Soprano looked hungry. I could see the hero wrapped up in tin foil, sticking out of a brown paper bag in his jacket pocket. I guess he couldn't eat it with all the rain.

Miss Della got everyone up to recite the philosophy. We stood in a circle and put our hands over each other's shoulders. I had Ivy on one side of me with Reggie on the other, and I felt safe between the two of them.

When we finished, Miss Della said, "Family, we talked a lot yesterday about what happened. But I know there are things we still need to say. We're all thankful that Clay is back with us. I want everyone to be respectful of what he's been through, and know that nobody here lost more than he did. If Clay isn't ready to talk about any part of this tragedy, I want family members to be respectful of that, too. Now, who needs to get something off their chest?"

"I just want to say fuck the *po*-lice," said Reggie. "Fuck 'em!"

"Control your language," Miss Della told her. "That shows discipline, and makes you even more powerful."

"They take that job just for the money, not to help people." Reggie got going again. "They're thugs. And if you're black they'll stick a bathroom plunger up your ass—Sorry, I mean up your rectum. They're worse than drug dealers."

"At least drug dealers don't pretend to be somebody else," said Ivy.

I thought about Henry giving Addison mouth to mouth. How maybe he was the last one to hold Addison while he was still alive. I wished I could be inside Henry's head and know for sure what he was thinking when Addison jumped out from behind that door, and how he felt right now.

"I'm gonna show people," said Reggie, pointing across the inside of her arm. "Then nobody will ever get me wrong. Everybody's gonna know straight off what I'm about."

"You wanna explain that to us?" Miss Della asked her.

"Not yet," said Reggie. "Right now, it's just for me to know."

"But it's a positive thing. It won't hurt anybody?" asked Miss Della.

"Trust me," answered Reggie. "All they're gonna have to do is read."

Angel said something in Spanish that took him almost two minutes to get out. He made his finger into a gun and let go of three popping noises.

"*Pop! Pop! Pop!*"

Everybody knew the word *policia*. We could tell from his voice and the look on his face how steamed he was. And when Angel was done, nobody had to ask Cruz to translate.

"One of those cops is black," said Latoya. "I don't understand that."

"Why, only white cops shoot people?" Tony asked quick.

"White or black, every cop wears blue. That makes 'em the biggest gang in New York City," said Ivy, folding her arms in front of her.

Miss Della gave a speech, saying how some of us would be old enough to vote in the next election for mayor. She said that we should take it serious if we wanted things to change.

"If there's some good to come out of this—maybe it'll unite the community behind the right candidate," said Miss Della.

"The mayor was at Addison's house yesterday," said Tony.

"So was Jackson Spiers," Miss Della said. "He'll be running for mayor, too."

It got quiet for a minute, and everybody had their eyes back on me. I put my head down and saw Addison's school folder under his desk.

"It's not right that he's dead just like that," I said, without thinking about it. "I know he wasn't perfect, but he didn't deserve what he got. We were just—"

There was a knock at the classroom door, and Andre stuck his head inside.

"Sorry to disturb the discussion, but I got one more family member," said Andre, letting in Clorox.

Andre pointed to the empty chair closest to the door, and Clorox sat down.

"Go on, Clay. Finish up," said Miss Della.

After that, I heard myself talking, but I couldn't

concentrate on the words. I took a deep breath and stared straight at Clorox. He dropped his eyes, so I stayed on the thin streak of white skin that started on his left cheek and went down to his lips, where it spread out over the bottom of his jaw.

"Wasn't that the roof to your building where everything happened, Warren?" Miss Della asked Clorox.

He nodded his head without looking up.

"You see staff finds out things like that," Miss Della told him. "You missed two consecutive days of program, including Guadenzia. Nobody answered your phone, so we sent a letter to your house. That's when we saw the addresses matched up. Is that why you weren't here yesterday?"

Clorox picked his eyes up fast, but they didn't settle on anybody.

He never answered, so Miss Della asked him, "Warren, how do you feel about what happened?"

"It's those lousy cops' fault," said Clorox into the top of his desk. "Nobody else's."

I wanted to pound his ass till he admitted his part in it, and I made a fist so hard that my knuckles turned white.

Andre came inside and said the family would be

meeting at six thirty to go to Addison's wake. I wondered if Clorox would show up and have the guts to look Addison in the face.

"We can't force anybody to go. But if you don't come I want to know why," Andre announced. "Obviously, Clay will be going with his own family."

We cleaned up breakfast and started school. I walked past Clorox to get my books and let my shoulder slam into his. He turned around, but never opened his mouth. On my way back, he put on his best ice-grill, but I stared straight through it, till it melted down to nothing.

I picked Addison's folder up off the floor and put it on my desk. The rain kept beating on the windows, and I watched the drops roll down the outside of the glass. Every couple of minutes, I'd turn around to shoot Clorox a look.

The first question in the GED practice book was about how the earth is always spinning. The drawing showed part of the world in sunlight, and the other part in shadows. They wanted me to figure out how long it took to change around. I went through the answers one by one, but none of them made any sense. Then I opened Addison's folder, and saw the fourth-grade reader. I stared at the picture of the boy playing fetch with his dog on the cover. And I wondered where that kid lived, because it wasn't part of any world I knew.

Clorox asked to use the bathroom, and Andre gave him the okay. A minute later, I told Andre I had to go, too. That it was a real emergency, and I couldn't wait for anybody to get back first.

I went down the stairs, past Miss Della's office. I shoved the bathroom door open, and Clorox was looking into the mirror over the sink.

"What? You gonna beat me down over a few bucks?" said Clorox, taking a roll of bills out of his pocket. "You're his family, so this passes on to you."

I just saw red.

I ripped the roll from his hand and pinned him against the sink.

"Is that what you think this is about?" I told him. "'Cause it's not. It's about your greedy ass getting Addison killed. And you know it!"

I wrapped a hand around Clorox's throat and squeezed till he couldn't breathe. When Clorox opened wide enough, I shoved the money into his mouth and slammed him to the floor.

Clorox spit out the roll, gasping for air. I looked at my hand, and it was still bent in the shape of his throat. But I didn't feel any better.

He sat on the floor, crying like he was six years old.

"I didn't mean for it to happen," said Clorox between sobs. "They did it! Those fucked-up cops killed him!"

His tears shook something inside of me. I could feel an earthquake starting at my toes and running up through my whole body. And I didn't want to pound him anymore, or prove anything to anybody.

Clorox wiped his eyes dry. Then he washed his face at the mirror till he was sure no one could tell he'd been crying.

He looked at the roll of bills on the floor, then back at me. But Clorox didn't move for it.

"And don't show up at that wake tonight," I told Clorox. "Addison's brother will wipe the fuckin' floor with you."

Clorox went back to class.

I stared hard into that same mirror. If I had a blunt in my hand, I would have fired it up for sure. And it probably would have been worth failing my next urine test just to numb everything inside me.

I picked up the money and buried it in my pocket.

At lunch, Reggie made a stink over Tony Soprano's sandwich.

"Look," said Reggie, pointing to Tony's pocket. "That hero's half the size it was this morning. He's been sneaking bites. That's against house rules."

Andre played it down and told Reggie to drop a slip on Tony if she was serious. Then he'd bring it up in group. Reggie wrote up a slip on the spot and dropped it into the complaint box. Tony didn't say a word back to her. He even had a smile on his face. But underneath, everybody knew that Tony was pissed.

There was plenty of food left over from Guadenzia. The macaroni and cheese my mom made was in a big yellow bowl. On the counter, I saw the aluminum tray Addison's mother brought to my house that night. Its sides were bent and pushed in, but there was still half a tray of ribs inside.

Clorox was at a table tearing into a rib. He had sweet sauce all over his mouth. But I couldn't touch one of those ribs now, and wouldn't even walk past the tray.

During group, Andre talked about how Addison's death could be pushing us to get high. Ivy said she felt it bad that night she went home from Guadenzia.

"I couldn't be alone, not with the liquor stores open," said Ivy slow. "So I slept with my mother in her bed, just to feel a warm body next to me."

I wanted to jump out of my chair and scream out how those feelings were burning inside of me. I could hear the words echo through my head. But I never opened my mouth. I pushed it back down, right on top of what I was hiding about Addison and the wallet. And I didn't want to go anywhere near either one of those things.

"I know some of you just aren't admitting it," Andre said, without looking right at me, "but if you can at least be honest with yourself, then that's a start. I've been clean for almost nine years now, and I'll tell you, Addison's death tested me. And I've got a lot more experience at staying sober than any of you. Remember, we're all the same here. To me, you're a sister or a brother from another mother. That's why this is a family."

Sometime during group, the rain finally quit. Before Andre sent us home, he told kids that Clorox wouldn't be going to Addison's wake. That he had a serious beef with somebody who'd be there.

"You probably already paid your respects to Clay this morning," Andre told Clorox. "But I'm sure you can give him a message to deliver to the rest of Addison's family."

"Just tell them I'm sorry, Clay," said Clorox. "Just that I'm sorry."

Outside, the sidewalk was full of branches and leaves that got knocked down by the storm. The gate to the tire shop was closed. That dog was way in the back, digging with both paws in the mud. I stopped in front of the fence to look. But he didn't care a thing about me. He was digging as fast as he could, like he needed to bury something where nobody would ever find it.

The wake was at Stallworth's Funeral Home that night. I didn't know any different, but my parents said it was the most expensive place in Queens. That Jackson Spiers got them to do it for free, and his limo was coming to pick us all up.

There must have been two hundred people waiting outside Stallworth's for the doors to open. But they let our family in first. Spiers and a preacher went with us. It was stone-quiet inside, and nobody talked above a whisper. I walked into the main room. There was nothing but flowers against two whole walls, reaching from the floor to the ceiling.

The lid to the coffin was open. From where I was standing, I could see the side of Addison's face. That was enough for me. After that, every time I got close, I kept my eyes turned away. And when nobody was watching, I had them shut.

Addison was dressed in a new suit that Spiers got him. A tailor even came down to the funeral home to measure him for it, and sewed it special in one day.

Addison's father came in the limo with us by himself. His other family showed up later with everybody else. He kept them away from Addison's mother, and things never got nasty.

All night, people came to pay their respects. Some were from the projects, but lots of them were strangers who wanted to say how wrong they thought Addison getting killed was. The mayor didn't come. But some regular white people off the street were there. And I give them props for walking into a room full of pissed-off black people when they didn't have to.

The family from Daytop came, and they mostly

stayed together. Andre and Miss Della talked for a while with Addison's mother, and then with Spiers.

I heard Addison's father introduce himself to the counselors. He shook their hands and said, "I want to thank you both from the bottom of my heart for trying to give my boy something better. It's so important what you do. Please, don't ever stop."

Reggie was acting jumpy and wouldn't go near Addison's coffin.

"I feel like dead people are watching you while you're looking at them. Only they see everything 'cause they're with God," said Reggie. "They know all your lies. That's why when my mother OD'd, I finally told myself the truth—that I was an addict like she was, and didn't know how to quit drugs."

So Reggie spent most of the time poking at Tony Soprano, threatening to point at him and scream out, "Klan!"

Ivy came back from kneeling at the casket and threw both arms around me. I could feel her tears on my cheek as she whispered into my ear, "I'm so sorry, Clay."

Operators who worked with Addison's mother came, too. They were all wearing pins that said 911—New York City Police Department. Darrel got superheated over that and tried to yank a pin off some man's jacket.

"Don't bring that shit in here! I don't want to see it!" screamed Darrel.

Somebody had to get in between to stop them from shoving at each other, and Darrel left, cursing at the man.

When it was time for the place to close, they had to make an announcement for people to leave. That's when Spiers took me off to a side room. He called my dad and the preacher in, too.

"After the funeral tomorrow, Clay, I want you come on *Black America* with me," said Spiers. "You need to let everyone know what really happened on that rooftop."

"I can't do—" I said, before he cut me off.

"You must!" said Spiers, bringing his teeth into my face. "It will get us the right kind of publicity, so that this crime doesn't go unpunished."

He took another step closer, and my back was almost against the wall. I could feel my heart pounding and the sweat starting at my forehead.

Then he took my arm, and pulled it out like I was holding a gun.

"It's time for you to shoot back, son!" Spiers

snarled. "You have to stand up and defeat what's keeping you down."

I tried to bounce, but Spiers grabbed me tight by the wrist. I pulled away and felt his nails dig into my skin, trying to hold on. Then I ran out the door, and I could hear my dad and the preacher trying to calm him down.

Out in the main room, I was alone with Addison. I walked up to the coffin and made myself look at him. He was lying there peaceful, like he was having some sweet dream. He was dressed in a sharp black suit with a white shirt and red tie. His hands were folded together on top of his stomach.

I didn't know how much he could really see, or what he'd think about me lying about the wallet. And I didn't know how I was supposed to reach Darrel for him.

The suit that Spiers got for Addison covered the bullet hole in his chest. But I didn't think anything in this whole world could cover up what was missing from inside of me.

CHAPTER 7

I TOOK THE stairs one at a time. I was working hard just to breathe, and every step was like going up the side of a mountain. It was dark, and cold as anything. I could feel the weight of the gun in my hand, and the badge pinned into my chest. Underneath me, the stairs started to give, and I knew there was nobody to catch me from behind. I could see the outline of the door to the roof. I knew it was a dream. That none of it was real. But I couldn't wake up.

The door flew open, and Addison jumped out. He was holding the biggest gun I'd ever seen, and it was pointed right at me.

He screamed, *"Bam! Bam!"*

His voice shot through me.

I tried to hold my finger back. But I just kept pulling the trigger.

I jerked up in my bed with both hands out in front of me. The muscles in my arms were tied up so tight, I could feel them burning all the way down to the tips of my fingers. Then I saw the shade pulled down over the window, and I started to breathe again.

It was five o'clock in the morning, and I didn't even try to get back to sleep. My dad was already awake. He was sitting at the kitchen table, going over the schedule for his laundry trucks.

"I can't sleep either," said Dad, lifting the pencil off the paper. "It's nothin' compared to everything else, but with Addison's funeral today I got to figure out how all this laundry is getting picked up and delivered without me or your uncle driving. Saturday's our busiest time. I swear, this world could stop cold, and some doctor or lab flunky would still be bitchin' that his coat isn't white enough."

It didn't matter that my dad was the boss. He worked six days a week, and almost never let up. Mom did all the billing from home and called the customers. Dad drove one of the routes and watched that the other drivers did their job right, too. Most of the stops were in medical offices. He'd haul off their dirty clothes and deliver the clean stuff on hangers, wrapped up in plastic.

People from around our way treated my dad like he was somebody special, because he made it out of the projects after dropping out of high school. He expected me to do even better, and get into college.

"You're movin' up from here, Clay. I'm not lettin' you slip back down into these streets," he told me a hundred times. "Getting some kind of college degree is gonna be part of that. One day folks will be talkin' 'bout everything *you* accomplished, not me."

Only I didn't know how I was going to climb up that high. And I was even more worried that I wouldn't get a foot off the ground.

I'd look at the elephant with the soap bubbles coming out of its trunk on the side of my dad's trucks and think, *No way I could ever be that big.*

"So they'll all spit fire if nobody shows up till Monday?" I asked him.

"People want to know their dirty laundry is

gone and out of sight, son. If they have to live with it for too long, it starts to eat away at them," said Dad, going back to his schedule.

By eight thirty we were all over at Addison's. My mom headed straight for their kitchen and started cooking pancakes and French toast for breakfast. Darrel wasn't there. His mother said he went outside someplace.

"Clay, please, go look for him," his mother said. "He can't be too far."

I found him on a side street, out behind his building. He was leaning up against the back end of a car, smoking a blunt. I wanted to turn and run, but I kept walking towards him anyway. Before he said a word, he held the blunt out for me to take a hit. I could smell the weed strong and see the smoke curling up around his hand.

"Not me," I said, trying to keep my voice steady. "The program will have my ass in a sling if my urine comes back positive."

"Just one pull for Addison," he said.

"I can't," I told him.

I was burning inside to smoke and had to wrestle hard against that part of me. I knew how easy I could get off the hook because of what happened to Addison. Everybody expected me to slip up. But I didn't want to play Addison's memory like that.

"And *I* don't want to get high," I finally said.

Then I thought about Darrel dealing crack and the look on Addison's face in the elevator that night. I wanted to say something to him about it, but I stopped to watch him take another hit.

"What the fuck is wrong with you two boys?" my uncle screamed, crossing the street to us. "Don't you understand that drugs helped kill Addison? So now you're gonna get high before his funeral?"

"Go worry about your real kids!" Darrel shouted back. "You know, the ones you see every damn day!"

"I screwed things up with your moms bad, but I never quit on being your father," he answered back. "Even when you quit on me, I tried to understand that. I sucked all that shit up, waiting for it to get better."

Then Darrel got up close to his father. He took a long pull from the blunt, and blew the smoke in his face.

Darrel started back to his building, and I was walking behind my uncle. When Darrel reached the front steps he turned around and said, "And Clay wasn't gettin' high. It was just me. That's what I do, 'cause I'm a grown man now!"

We got inside, and Darrel was already on the stairs. His father pressed the elevator button, and I waited with him. On the ride up, he said with his voice shaking, "I care about all my children, Clay. I don't want to bury any more of them."

Darrel had a plate in his hand and was reaching across the table for the pancakes when we walked in.

"I'll ask you again, Darrel. Where did you disappear to?" his mother said.

"It's all right. Leave him be!" his father took up for him. "He was with me, explaining how it is to be a man."

I thought he'd give Darrel up for sure, but he didn't.

And I could see the worried look leave Darrel's face.

"But we're gonna finish that talk soon," his father said. "You're wrong on certain things. And that's all I'm gonna say for now!"

Spiers's limo took us to Stallworth's. He didn't say a word to me, and that whole ride I kept looking at the marks he'd left on my wrist.

By ten o'clock, the funeral home was mobbed.

There were folding chairs set up all the way to the back wall, and every one of them was filled. Spiers sat in the front row with our family. Right behind us were black leaders I'd seen on TV from Harlem, Brooklyn, and the Bronx.

Addison's mother had a black veil over her face, and so did my mom. The coffin was closed this time, and I stared at the light shining off the brown-and-black wood. The preacher wore black pants and a black shirt with a white collar around his neck. There was a microphone hooked up to a wooden stand with an African flag hanging from it. The preacher tapped the mike with his finger, and when the sound bounced off the walls, he started his speech. He said his piece about God and heaven, and how dying wasn't the end of everything. Then he tugged at his collar, and his face and voice got harder.

"Addison Reynolds didn't create the society in which we live. Sadly, he didn't live long enough to help change it. But what happened to him can't help but shape the way we live in this city. Addison lived in the Ravenswood Houses. And in this society, that can start you out from a long way behind. The school system failed to meet his needs as he struggled with a learning disability. And as with too many of our children who are confronted by a sense of hopelessness, Addison was seduced by the streets. Thankfully, he survived that mistake. Addison found his way into a program addressing his personal problems and educational needs. Then all of that was taken from him.

"There's little doubt that the color of his skin caused the death of Addison Reynolds. I don't know what it is about the sight of our people that stirs a sense of hatred and fear in so many so-called peace officers. But it must come to an end.

"Brothers and sisters, I call upon you to never close your eyes, to speak the truth, and to hide nothing out of fear. I can assure you that Addison's soul is among us now, waiting for the truth to be told. For only the light of truth, no matter how difficult to face, will lead us from this terrible darkness. Amen!"

Everybody started clapping and wouldn't stop. And for two or three minutes, there were voices shouting, "Amen!"

I knew part of the truth was locked up inside of me. I didn't know if it would ever find a way out, or how things would come back on me if it did, but that hole in the middle of my chest had stopped aching. And I started to believe that if I faced up to everything staring me down, it might even close up one day.

Spiers was the first one out of his seat to shake the preacher's hand. He wrapped an arm around him and faced the crowd. His eyes caught mine for a second, but I didn't turn my head an inch. And I felt like I could see straight through him.

Maybe Spiers cared about everything he said he did, but I knew he was propping up his chances of being mayor on what my family was going through. And I almost hoped that he wouldn't win.

There were three of us on each side of Addison's casket. We lifted it up and carried it out to the hearse. Addison's father and Darrel held the handles on the front end, Andre and Spiers were in the middle, and me and my dad were together at the back.

A long line of cars left Stallworth's for the cemetery. The police stopped traffic to start us out, but everybody honked their horns at them to leave. The hearse circled the neighborhood and rode by the Ravenswood Houses. I felt every bump and pothole on those streets. We came up on Clorox's building, and Addison's mother said through her tears, "I'll have to live with walking past there every day for the rest of my life."

We passed Addison's building and turned up the street where I live. Then the hearse headed back around. It wasn't even noon, and there was already a dealer doing business on the corner. I looked over at Darrel and knew I had to push him off the idea of selling crack.

All the cars with us had their headlights on and stayed together. Nothing split them up, and they rolled through red lights like they weren't there.

At the cemetery, we walked up a steep grass hill. There was a six-foot-deep hole with fresh dirt piled up high on the side. The workers lowered Addison's casket into the ground. The preacher said a few more words about God. Then everybody took a turn dropping a handful of dirt into the grave.

When Miss Della got her turn, she told people, "This is from the philosophy Addison said every morning at Daytop: 'Fearing not the solitude of death, but rejoicing in my love for others.'"

I dug my hand deep into the pile. Then I looked down at the top of Addison's casket and felt the dirt slip through my fingers. The casket was just starting to get covered. But we couldn't come close to filling up that hole by ourselves. And the workers stood on the side with shovels, waiting for us to finish.

The ride home was hard, and even my dad broke down bawling for a minute. Addison's father was sobbing, too, before he left with his other family. I shut my eyes and forced my cheeks up high, but I was still bone-dry inside. So I buried my face in both hands and sucked air through my mouth till it almost felt like I was crying.

That afternoon, the police put out their report. It was all over the radio and TV news. Watisick killed Addison. The tests on his gun and the bullet they pulled out of Addison proved it. He squeezed off two shots, and one of them hit Addison in the chest. I turned numb when I heard it for the first time. But somewhere down deep, I was glad it wasn't Henry.

I had to hear it twice before I caught on that the police department was giving them all a free pass and said there was nothing wrong with what they did. And that only the DA could step in now and file charges against them.

"Again, just in to the newsroom—all three officers

in the Addison Reynolds shooting, acquitted of departmental charges. The officers will receive their guns and badges back. However, they are expected to be transferred to other precincts, confirms a high-ranking police source. Queens District Attorney Dennis Wolf is expected to review the case for possible state charges, and release a statement soon."

The report said the cops already had their guns out, going up the last set of stairs. That it was legal because rooftops in the projects are so dangerous. Nevin was walking up front. He said Addison surprised him, and that he saw something in his hand. Then Nevin told them that he tripped, and his gun went off by accident.

There was a metal frame around the door. And the report said Nevin's shot hit that, and the bullet probably ricocheted back at the cops. They thought Addison was shooting at them, and fired. Henry was standing behind Watisick, and took one shot. It was only the second time Henry had ever pulled the trigger on patrol.

Dad was cursing over it, and kicked a hole through the back of a kitchen chair.

"These sons of bitches are tellin' stories to back each other up! Fuckin' lies—lies they couldn't get away with if they weren't cops!" he said into the air, walking right past me.

My stomach was churning hot. I hated every damn bit of what I heard. But something small inside me was breathing easier, and said my lie about the wallet didn't matter now. That Henry and those bastards couldn't get fucked over because of it. That's when the puke shot into my mouth. I swallowed it back down. But I could still taste it and feel it burning my throat.

The phone rang. It was my mom at Addison's, and we got over there quick. There was already a TV truck setting up outside. Spiers's bone-crusher was at the end of the hall, and two reporters, who couldn't get past him, were over by the stairs.

"As family members, what's your reaction to the report?" one of them yelled at us.

"If I told you how I *really* felt, you couldn't print it," Dad answered. "Not in a newspaper."

There weren't any tears inside that apartment. Maybe Addison's mother had cried herself out over everything that happened before. She was angrier than anyone I'd ever seen. But she wasn't scream-ing or cursing, or punching walls. Instead, her face had turned rock-solid. And her eyes looked like they were glued to something in front of her the rest of us couldn't see.

"First, the police commissioner said it was wrong, but *now* it's okay. I don't care what I have to do, but that DA's gonna stand up for what's right and bring charges against these bastards," said Addison's mother, without blinking.

Dad tightened the lid on his temper in front of my aunt and mom. But Darrel was out of control, and couldn't hold back.

"He tripped, my ass! It took 'em three days to think up that ricochet bullshit! That's why you don't walk a straight line in the hood. 'Cause when you do, they just change things around," roared Darrel. "All I know is the city sent that white moth-erfucker to the projects to kill my brother!"

My mom said the DA was a black dude with kids of his own. That he wouldn't be able to show his face in front of his own people if he let the cops slide.

"He don't care," said Darrel. "He got to be an Oreo cookie to hold that job, black on the outside and white on the inside."

"I won't allow it to be like that!" his mother said.

Darrel was ready to run his mouth again, but my dad put two hands on his shoulders to slow him down. Then Darrel looked at his mother and took a deep breath. But he couldn't stop himself.

"The cops can't tell me shit anymore, 'cause I ain't listenin'. One day, I'm gonna be big enough to own these streets and them, too," Darrel exploded, slamming his bedroom door behind him.

"Lord, keep me strong enough to stand up to this, and save the only son you left me," prayed his mother.

Black America started that afternoon with the clip of the police commissioner saying, "The shooting appears totally unjustified." Then they cut to the film of some other top cop reading the report, with the mayor and police commissioner standing behind him. After he read the part about how the cops were in the clear with them, the show played the commissioner's words from the first clip over and over again, making the picture blurry with the words fading out like an echo.

"The shooting appears totally unjustified . . . appears totally unjustified . . . totally unjustified . . . unjustified . . . unjustified."

Spiers was in the studio live with the host of the show, blasting the report.

"It's hard to believe, but in New York City, it's appropriate police procedure for officers to have their guns drawn while on 'vertical patrol,'" Spiers said, making the quotation marks in the air with two fingers on each hand. "And that phrase simply means going up the stairs to the roof. The police want you to believe that the rooftops are a wild jungle of crime. Of course, in reality, there's only one reason it's allowed—because ninety-nine-point-nine percent of the people living in city housing projects aren't white. And if it wasn't that way, it wouldn't be tolerated."

The mayor came on the show, too. Only he wasn't really there. He was on a TV monitor. He said how sorry he was about Addison, and that now it was up to the DA to decide. That the law would take its course.

"Did you see the face of your police commissioner while that report was being read, Mr. Mayor?" said Spiers. "His eyes were on the floor because he knows it was wrong. He said so. But now he's got to jump through hoops for you. When are you going to stand up for what's right, and start being mayor to all the people of this city?"

"You're trying to turn this into something political," the mayor shot back. "I'm not going to do that."

"Why not?" growled Spiers. "It's the politics of inequality that got Addison Reynolds killed. And it's politics trying to take away all responsibility for it. So why shouldn't this be political?"

Then Spiers said how police in New York City have forty-eight hours before they have to give a written statement whenever they fire their guns.

"That's long enough to get everybody tellin' the same story," said Spiers. "And it's one of the first things I'll work to change when I'm mayor."

Twice as many cops were on the streets around the Ravenswood Houses that night. There was even an armor-plated police bus parked on one corner in case there was a riot. But things mostly stayed quiet.

A TV reporter was on the rooftop, talking to people about how they felt. The camera showed all the candles burning by the door where Addison got shot. I could look at the TV with one eye and outside my window with the other and see the same light shining in two places at once.

Mom and Dad didn't go to the roof yet.

"It's where I almost lost you, Clay," my mom said. "Jesus knows, I'm just not ready to see it with my own eyes."

Addison's mother said that she couldn't go up there till somebody paid for what they did to her son. And I wasn't sure if I ever wanted to set foot on that black tar again.

CHAPTER 8

LATE THAT NIGHT, somebody dropped a bowling ball off the roof where Addison got killed. There were two cops standing outside, in front of the building. The news said the bowling ball hit right between them. That they dove for cover, thinking they were getting shot at with a cannon. An army of cops searched up and down the building, but whoever did it got away clean.

There were orange cones tied together with yellow tape that read CAUTION on the four corners of the cement block the bowling ball slammed into. It left a crater maybe six inches deep, and would have crushed somebody's skull like an egg. Lots of people walking past stopped to see. I stared at the hole for a long time, and tried to figure how much force it took to break through something that solid. And I knew that even after they filled that hole in with new cement, nobody around here would ever look at it the same.

When I walked into Daytop on Monday, Angel's horse was gone from over the inside door. It didn't hit me till I saw the Scotch tape still on the wall. Andre was on the phone in his office, and one of the horse's legs was sticking up from out of the garbage can. After that, I didn't want to look. So I put my head down and got past it fast as I could.

Reggie was upstairs, wiping the inside of her arm with rubbing alcohol. She had the word SINCERE tattooed across it in big letters.

"See! I told you I was gonna represent and let everybody know," Reggie said. "This is how I wanna be—'sincere,' even when the shit around me isn't, like that bullshit report the cops put out."

Tony Soprano laughed at Reggie's new ink, and said she'd never spell the ending of a business letter wrong again.

"That's sincerely," Reggie told him. "That has an L-Y, like for the way you always lie."

Clorox wasn't there, and that was all right by me. I didn't want to see his face, or hear how much money he was making dealing drugs.

Andre and Miss Della ran morning meeting together. They both said how flipped they were over the cops getting off the hook for now, and knew that everybody felt the same. When it was time to read the newspaper, Andre asked if we wanted to skip the headlines and just stick to the horoscopes and weather. Then we wouldn't have to keep hearing about the report. Kids voted a hundred percent to do it that way, and so did the counselors.

"We're not pretending it didn't happen," Miss Della said. "But if I want to read fairy tales, I'll stick to *Little Red Riding Hood*. At least I know for sure the wolf gets what's coming to him in the end."

Then Andre said that Clorox wasn't here because he got arrested selling drugs the day before. That he'd probably blow probation and be locked up for a few years.

"Warren didn't have the confidence in himself to leave certain things behind. His urines showed us that," said Andre, shaking his head. "I don't like to use people as negative examples. He's still a family member, and I hope he gets treatment. But you gotta change! You gotta grow! That's why we're here!"

I knew Andre was right. That Clorox had real problems and needed help. But I was still happy to see Clorox get his.

When school started, Miss Della took Ivy, Tony Soprano, and me into the kitchen where it was quiet. She pulled out the GED predictor test and gave us the booklets for the parts we still needed to pass. Then she sat us at different tables, with our backs to each other.

"I'm all for family members helping each other, but there are some mountains you gotta climb for yourself. This test right here is just one of them," Miss Della said, checking her watch.

Ivy and Tony just had the social studies part to do. I had to take the science and the math.

I tried to clear my head of everything else, but I couldn't. And I had to fight hard to stay focused. There were only a few different practice tests, so I'd seen a lot of the questions already. Sometimes I knew the answer before I even looked at the choices. I got on a good run in the beginning of the science section, and I knew I had enough answers right to coast from there.

Ivy finished first and asked Miss Della to grade it on the spot.

"I need to know my score now," said Ivy. "I'd be too nervous waiting to find out."

She was jumping up and down with every check-mark Miss Della put on her paper.

"That's eighteen right already. I pass!" screamed Ivy, giving Miss Della a high five.

Ivy got twenty-one out of twenty-five right and passed easy. Tony was sweating over his test and got bent out of shape over the noise Ivy made cele-brating. But he handed his test in just after I got started on the math.

Tony stood over Miss Della as she went down his answers.

"If I fail don't say the score out loud," Tony told her.

"Why, is there some kinda shame in tryin' your best?" Miss Della asked without getting an answer.

I watched Tony pull tight and say something under his breath every time he got one wrong. But in the end, Tony squeaked by. He smacked his hands together loud and headed back to the classroom.

"You've got almost a half hour left, Clay. Call me, and I'll come back to check both your papers," Miss Della said, leaving me alone.

In between questions, I started thinking how Addison and me never made it to Guadenzia that night. How we should have been here, watching Ivy and her mother do their dance. Instead, we were out chasing after Clorox, like two idiots.

I had a handle on most of the math, and I got to the end with about ten minutes to spare. Then I went back to redo the ones I'd guessed at.

Dad told me how they got the news about Addison and me. They were setting up the food inside this kitchen, worried sick about where we were. They thought maybe we got into a beef with some kids on the way over, or some other kind of trouble. When the cops walked in, everybody figured we got arrested for something, maybe even drugs.

The cops only told them that one of us got shot. My parents and Addison's mother freaked out over which one of us it was. They were holding hands, praying together that we'd both be all right.

"Son, what I was really asking God was that it wouldn't be you," Dad told me when we were alone. "When I found out it was your cousin, I never felt so relieved *and* ashamed. And when I hugged your mother, I could feel it inside of her, too."

When they got the news that Addison was killed, Dad said he wanted to crawl down a sewer somewhere and never come back up.

There was a black circle inside a much bigger white one. I had to figure out how much area was left in just the white part of the circle. It was one of the hardest questions on the whole test. Andre said he didn't know how to teach that problem and wouldn't even put it on the board in class. There weren't any answers to pick from, either, and I had to come up with one on my own. I erased my answer so many times, I almost put a hole in the paper.

I looked over at the table where I first saw Addison sitting with his back to me. In my head, I could see his shoulders standing out from everybody else's, and the brown #32 jersey he was wearing.

The circle question had me totally stumped. I didn't feel like guessing anymore, so I left it blank. I crumpled up my scrap paper and chucked it into the trash. Then I went to find Miss Della. I passed both tests, and she scheduled all three of us to take the real GED exam in a couple of weeks.

Later on, we were in the middle of group with Miss Della when Andre interrupted.

"I thought you'd all like to know. I just heard on the radio—the district attorney is gonna ask a grand jury to indict Watisick . . . the one who shot Addison," he said, with a head of steam. "The charge is gonna be second-degree manslaughter. I don't know all the specifics of what that means, but he could get up to fifteen years in prison."

Right away, my insides were on a roller-coaster ride. I could feel everything turning upside down and out of control. I wanted that bastard to pay for what he did to Addison. But now I had to stress over what my lie about the wallet would do to him in court.

Cruz was in the middle of translating when Angel said, "Fif-teen," flashing all his fingers, then just the ones on his right hand.

"That's it?" asked Reggie. "He can't get the death penalty or anything?"

"Unfortunately, that's not how the system works," Miss Della answered.

"What about those other two cops?" Reggie wanted to know.

"Nothing, I guess," said Andre.

"Do *you* think that's justice, Clay?" Ivy asked.

I shook my head, but I wasn't sure what that word meant anymore.

On the way out, I lifted my eyes enough to look in the garbage for Angel's horse. Only it was gone, and the can was empty. Latoya probably bagged it up and took it out to the street with the rest of the trash during structure.

Mom made stew for us to take over to Addison's mother that night. She had the news on from the second I came home, listening to every report about what the DA was going to do. Addison's mother called, and they listened to some of the stories together. And when my dad got home, he was pumped over the news, too.

I told my parents about me taking the GED, and they were proud as anything over it.

"Please, Clay, don't mention it in front of your aunt," Mom said. "She'll only feel even worse thinkin' 'bout all the things Addison never got a chance to do."

On the walk over, I saw Darrel on the opposite corner. It looked like he was hanging out, but I knew better by the guys he was with. I told my parents I wanted to see if he was coming up to eat, and crossed over.

"So the DA came through a little bit," said Darrel, giving me a pound. "But I'll believe it when I see that cop's ass behind bars."

I told him about Clorox getting locked up for selling, and he just smiled. Then I mentioned the roll of bills I had that belonged to his brother.

"And, Darrel," I said, taking a long breath, "Addison was real worried 'bout you dealin'. He didn't want you doin'—"

But Darrel only heard the part about the money, and cut me off.

"So how much is there?" he asked.

A car pulled up, and Darrel said he had to take care of business. But I wouldn't wait around, and left.

Addison's mother had a candle burning in her window. She gave another one to my dad, and he said he'd bring it up to the roof for her soon.

They were talking about the DA going after Watisick, and if it was right for Henry and Nevin to get off free.

"As long as somebody pays, I'll be satisfied," said Addison's mother. "I feel those other two didn't shoot my boy, so they weren't gonna get convicted anyway. The DA knows what he's doing. He went after the one he could get indicted the easiest."

"And since Henry's not being charged, the DA can go after what this really is: a white cop shooting an unarmed black kid," said Dad.

And both my mom and aunt backed him up on that.

"They already have your statement, but they could still call you in front of that grand jury, Clay," Mom said.

"If they do, you just tell them the way it happened," said Addison's mother. "That's all anybody can ask."

All through dinner, we were watching the news on TV. Spiers came on from City Hall, saying how the DA got it right. That only the mayor didn't want to see things how they really were.

"God bless that man for everything he's done," said my aunt.

Then Spiers stared straight into the camera. He opened his mouth wide, and all I could see were his teeth.

"Maybe justice is supposed to be blind, but not our elected leaders," said Spiers. "I don't close my eyes on anything, or anybody!"

I went to bed early that night, but my eyes

wouldn't keep shut. By eleven o'clock, my mom and dad were both sound asleep. I went into the kitchen and saw the candle that Addison's mother gave my dad lying on the table. Then I went back to my bed-room window and looked at the light coming off the roof. I felt a spark inside of me start to catch. So I got dressed quick and headed out the door with that candle.

There was a police car parked on the corner, but I passed by it without a second thought.

I walked around Clorox's building twice before I got the courage to start up the front steps. The crater from where the bowling ball slammed the concrete was still there. Only this time I didn't look into the hole; I was staring straight up at the black sky instead.

I started up in the elevator, and felt the weight of everything pushing down on me. Then the metal doors sprung open, and I could see the stairs to the roof. They were narrow, and only lit up halfway. And from the bottom, the door at the top was just a shadow. I put all my weight on the first step, and when my legs didn't buckle, I sprinted the rest of the way up with my eyes closed.

I steadied myself at the top and tried to slow

down my breathing. That door was maybe a foot from my face and felt like it was closing in on top of me. The metal frame had dents and scratches all around it. But I couldn't pick out the place where the report said Nevin's shot ricocheted. I didn't want to be buried in that one spot my whole life, so I pushed the door open fast, and stepped onto the roof.

His eyes were fixed on mine. He was standing next to where Addison got killed, and I could see his face in the light from the candles.

"Tell me right now if we're gonna have some sort of problem," Henry said low.

I shook my head and stood next to him, with his shoulders twice the size of mine.

"I replayed every one of those shots ten thousand times in my mind," said Henry, staring into the light. "And I still don't know how it turned out like this."

For a while, there was nothing but the sound of the wind, and cars from the street. Every feeling in the world was running through me. They were shoving each other back and forth, and I wasn't sure which one would win, or come flying out first.

"I don't hate you anymore," I finally said. "I thought I did, but I don't. I can't say that about those other two cops"

I watched the wax dripping down the candles, turning hard again in a little hill at the bottom. The flames were burning yellow over red, and I squeezed the candle inside my hand tight.

"In my projects, growin' up, the cops slapped kids around like they were nobody. And I'd run every time I saw one comin'. I could never figure how I came to put on that uniform. But I swore it would be different with me," Henry said. "And if that's changed any, I got to search inside why."

Then Henry looked out over the project buildings and said he was getting transferred because of the shooting.

Deep down, I knew I was stealing something important from him by not telling the truth about that night. And maybe I was robbing the whole Ravenswood Houses, too.

"You just let his mother know for me that I'm sorry," Henry said.

I didn't say anything back to him, and just stared at my feet on the tar floor.

I finally bent down to set up the candle for Addison's mother. There was a big box of wooden matches that somebody left behind. I slid it open, and struck one against the black edge of the box. The yellow flame jumped from my hand to the candle, and I blew the match out.

When I turned back around, Henry had already disappeared down the stairs.

CHAPTER 9

THE NEXT MORNING, the guy who runs the tire shop was washing down the yard with a hose. He had his thumb over the nozzle, spraying water up into the air. That dog was panting hard, going back and forth trying to catch the drops in his mouth. The guy was all smiles over it, and finally let the dog drink straight from the hose. Then he rubbed him underneath his neck till the dog rolled over onto his back, barking like an innocent puppy. And anybody walking past that yard for the first time probably would have wanted to stop and play with that dog, too.

When I got to Daytop, I went upstairs to the kitchen and almost couldn't believe it. Bell was sitting there eating breakfast, like he never got shipped upstate.

"But you went to residential," I said.

"It was too crazy for me, Clay," said Bell.

"They just let you leave?" I asked him.

"Let me? No!" he answered. "I packed all my shit and just started walking. They didn't even know I was gone, at first. I walked by the side of the highway. I made it almost twelve miles before the cops came."

"They didn't arrest you or anything?" I asked.

"For what, walking?" answered Bell. "They already knew who I was. They even called me by my name. I just told them I wasn't goin' back. That they couldn't make me. It's all gang nonsense in there. If you're not down with the right crew, they try to make you into a slave."

Bell said he told the counselor upstate that he'd just walk out again. Then he said his mother got on the phone and cursed out the counselor for letting him disappear that way, so they put him on the next bus home.

"I heard about Addison while I was up there. I was like, *I was just with him and his cousin at Daytop.* A couple of guys there knew him, too," Bell said. "I was thinkin' about him every step I took by that highway. And when the cops rolled up on me, I took my hands out of my pockets and held them out to the side, so they wouldn't think I had a gat."

Bell asked how I got the news about Addison. That's when I told him I was on the roof with him.

"That was you in between all those bullets?" Bell said. "Damn! You lucky to be alive, Clay. God must have a plan for you."

Reggie came in, ragging on Bell for getting his ass whipped upstate.

"They can't let you back in this program now," Reggie told Bell.

"I don't know. My mother's comin' to see Andre and Miss Della today," said Bell. "They have to talk to my PO, too. I haven't had any weed in a week. I think I'm cured."

"You ain't cured!" Reggie shouted. "You just scared shitless for your urine to be dirty again."

Then Bell wanted to know where Clorox was.

"The same place you'll be if your PO hates on you," said Reggie.

"Word? He's locked up?" said Bell. "Everything's changin' around."

At morning meeting, the counselors skipped

the weather and horoscopes and went straight to the news stories. They had two different newspapers, and Ivy and me took turns reading stories about the DA going after Watisick.

"Queens District Attorney Dennis Wolf will ask a grand jury to indict first-year Officer Richard Watisick for second-degree manslaughter in the rooftop shooting death of Addison Reynolds, an unarmed teen previously convicted of drug dealing," Ivy read, stopping a second to keep from crying.

"Why'd they have to say that—'convicted of drug dealing'?" Reggie asked out loud, slapping a hand down on her desk.

"Because that's the way they are," said Miss Della, before she looked at Ivy and asked, "Do you need me to finish, dear?"

But Ivy didn't answer and started reading again. "Watisick could face a maximum penalty of fifteen years in prison if convicted. A report issued by the police department's Firearms Discharge Review Board cleared Watisick of any wrongdoing. Initially, Police Commissioner Charles Lieber had called the shooting 'unjustified.' It is believed that Reynolds, who held a black wallet in his hand, and may have been trying to show his ID, surprised a trio of officers at a door leading to a rooftop in the Ravenswood Houses. A charge of second-degree manslaughter requires that a defendant be aware of the risks of loss of life, but display a disregard for them.

"DA Wolf stated, 'I consider this to be a clear-cut case of an officer using deadly force as an extreme overreaction to only a possible threat. We've seen too many instances of those living in our poorest neighborhoods not being afforded that right. On Park Avenue, a wallet's always a wallet. It's never a gun. It should be that way in our city housing projects, too.'"

Cruz leaned in over Ivy's shoulder to get a better look at the picture.

"Yo, that's the DA? That skinny black dude with the glasses? That's the guy everybody with a case against them is afraid of?" asked Cruz.

"He don't have to be brolic," Bell said. "He got the courts on his side for muscle."

Angel told Cruz that wasn't the guy who showed up against him in court. Then Andre explained how the DA handles only big cases, and his assistants work on the small ones.

"You don't ever want to see *that* guy," said Tony. "That means you're fucked big-time."

"He goes after mafia people, like your family on *The Sopranos*," Cruz said.

"No, like your boy from *Scarface*—Tony Montana," Tony shot back, grinning.

That's when Andre gave a speech about stereotypes, and said it was the same kind of thinking that probably got Addison killed.

I didn't want to hear any more about that, so I started reading fast.

"Officer Richard Watisick, who resides in the quiet Long Island suburb of Melville, far removed from the inner-city neighborhoods he patrols, is at the center of a racial firestorm. Watisick, a husband and father of two young children, could soon be indicted on a charge of second-degree manslaughter in the shooting death of an unarmed African-American teenager, Addison Reynolds, on a housing-project rooftop." I stopped to swallow.

Watisick didn't say a word for himself in the story. His lawyer did all the talking. He said how Watisick got treated for trauma after the shooting and couldn't sleep for days. Then I thought about

Addison's mother, and what right that bastard had to feel the same way. If he really did, and it wasn't just a show to stay out of jail.

Henry was free and clear. He didn't kill anybody. But at least Henry had it in him to say he was sorry.

"My client feels it's a tragedy," Watisick's lawyer said. "One the circumstances made unavoidable."

Then the lawyer said how Watisick would probably have to quit the police department and start a new life. That the police commissioner told the whole world how Watisick screwed up before he knew all the facts. And that no matter where the city sent him to patrol, people on the street would hassle him every day.

Even if I wasn't telling the whole truth about what happened, at least Watisick had a life to go back to. Addison didn't have a damn thing anymore, except the suit that Spiers dressed him up in.

The last part of the story was about how Watisick's best friend from high school was black, and how they were on the track team together.

"Richard Watisick has never been hateful towards African-Americans," his friend told the paper. "I know that whatever happened that night had nothing to do with the color of anybody's skin."

My eyes stayed on the picture of Watisick mowing his lawn with a black dog following behind him.

"I bet that black guy got paid to pretend he was his best friend," said Latoya.

"Maybe that cop's all right with black people from Long Island," Bell said. "They all got money and mostly act white anyway."

Ivy finished up by reading a story about Spiers. He said that he'd tear down the "Blue Wall of Silence" one brick at a time if he had to, no matter how much cement the mayor gave the cops to use.

Kids never heard of any wall before, so Andre explained what Spiers meant.

"The Blue Wall of Silence is where the cops stick together, no matter what. If one of them does something wrong, the others lie for him, or say they didn't see it. Their stories are always exactly the same, and they never go against each other," said Andre.

"Like that first cop, Nevin, saying he tripped and that his gun went off by accident. And then the ricochet," Ivy said. "That all fits together too perfect."

"They're lucky that Clay was on the *other* side of that door, or else they'd have to tell the truth," said Reggie.

"They coulda told the same story and just said that Clay was lyin'," said Latoya.

"Lyin' 'bout what?" Bell came back. "Like Addison was gonna shoot it out against three cops with his wallet!"

I listened to it all and wondered what color wall I was hiding behind. Then I felt for the hole in the middle of my chest, and knew where some of the bricks I used were from.

After lunch, I was mopping the kitchen floor and hallway for structure. Ivy came upstairs with her clipboard and told Tony Soprano that he was doing a shitty job cleaning the classroom. I finished with the mop and went in to check it out. The classroom looked all right to me. But I walked over to the shelves and stood the books up on their side, the way Addison used to do. Then Tony started doing the same on the other side of the room. Ivy came back in and froze for a few seconds, like a statue.

"Any better now, chief?" Tony asked her.

She nodded her head and turned back around.

That night, I saw Darrel doing business out on the corner again. I watched him and the guys he was with sell to one dude who looked like a bag of bones and couldn't even walk straight. I finally went over and tried to talk to Darrel on the side, but the animals with him kept barking, "This ain't no family hour!" So I told him I had something important and asked him to meet me in the playground behind his building the next day, after I got through with Daytop.

- - - - -

Darrel was there ahead of me, hanging with one of the guys who worked the corner. They were standing inside the monkey bars. Darrel was finishing a set of chin-ups, and the other dude was sparking up a joint.

"None for my cuz, dog. He's in rehab," said Darrel, taking a hit from the joint. "But that don't matter. He's my boy forever. He came off that roof and told everybody how those lyin' cops *really* did my brother."

I smelled the weed, but I wasn't fiending for it. Not now. Then I saw that Darrel had Addison's diamond studs in his ears, and I couldn't hold back another second.

"Darrel, that night Addison got killed, he told me how worried he was for you," I said. "He didn't know how to say it, but he didn't want you playin' the corner, dealin' crack. He knew everything that happened to him would jump up and bite you, too."

"That's what you got me out here for—some sermon?" he said, sucking his teeth at me. "Man, I thought you had money that belonged to my brother for me. Not this bullshit!"

I said, "Listen, you can't risk everything on—"

"Risk what?" he cut me off, wrapping his arms around the bars. "I got nothin' to lose. You got a father with do-re-mi—money. He's got trucks with his name on the side, so that's what *you* got, too. It's all my mother can do to pay the rent. And I'm in line behind my pop's other set of kids for shit. So I found a way to set myself up at the front of the line, the same way Addison did."

"You don't have to find yours on the corner," I said, looking at him through the bars. "You got more than that inside of you."

"They took part of what I had when they snatched up my brother. Now those motherfuckers

owe me somethin','" Darrel said, with a hard look.
"You're clean! You walked off that rooftop like an
angel. Why don't you go hang with Jackson Spiers?
You're down with him now. Go make everything
right for everybody else. I'll still be lookin' for
mines on the corner!"

Then Darrel ducked under the monkey bars and
headed out of the yard. The other dude snuffed out
his smoke and followed behind him.

"How 'bout that roll of greenbacks you had for
me?" Darrel said, turning back around. "When do I
collect on that, cuz?"

"The next time I see you, I'll bring it," I told
him. "I don't want any part of it."

I walked away knowing I really *was* down with
Spiers, and that made me sick.

When I got back home, I took the roll of bills out
of my dresser drawer and felt the weight of it in my
hand. It was almost nothing, but it cost Addison
his life. And I wondered—if I threw it out the window, would it split the sidewalk in two?

CHAPTER 10

ADDISON'S MOTHER USED up the days her job allowed for a funeral, and her sick time, too. Halfway through her first shift back at work, she took off her headset and walked away from the phones. She said that she couldn't stop shaking. That she went into the bathroom, and sat in one of the stalls, and cried.

"It wasn't the calls where somebody needed an ambulance or there was a fire," she said. "But the ones where somebody saw something and wanted the cops to come right away. I kept thinking how they might go there and shoot someone dead, like they did my baby."

Spiers said he'd talk to somebody at City Hall about getting her transferred off the 911 hotline. But that he couldn't promise anything because the mayor and his people might not be in the mood to do him or us any favors.

I knew Addison's mother already had too much to deal with, so I wouldn't go to her about Darrel. But if Darrel got locked up or worse, I didn't know how she could handle it. Then I thought about my uncle and everything I'd seen him do since Addison told me how he wouldn't open the door for him that night. So I found my mom's phone book and wrote out his number.

Ivy went through all the math books at Daytop and finally found one that explained how to do the problem with the black circle inside the white one. During math time, Miss Della taught the rest of the kids easier stuff, and Andre sat at a table in the back with Ivy, Tony, and me, practicing how to get that problem right.

"You all know I'm not a real math teacher," said Andre. "I thought once I got outta school, balancing a checkbook would be the most I ever had to deal with. But I guess not."

It felt all right to hear an adult admit that he didn't know something and sit down next to me and try to learn it from the beginning. Andre had a lot of pull over what happened to kids at Daytop.

Only he'd stand right up and say that he was an addict, too, and that he was no better than anybody else here. That he was just older and had more experience at getting things done. But when it came to figuring out how much more space was inside the white circle, Andre was lost like the rest of us.

Over the next couple of days, we spent an hour every morning working on that one problem. I even copied everything out of the book by hand and studied it at home. I had to find the area of both circles, then take the black one away from the white one. The formula uses pi. And pi never changes. It stays the same, no matter what size the circles get to be.

Tony Soprano thought he had it figured out. He wrote the answer down on a piece of paper and left it in the middle of the table. Andre checked Tony's answer in the back of the book, and he was right. Tony put a big grin on his face and made us all sweat him to tell us how he did it. But soon as he said it out loud, Ivy got it right away. Then she showed Andre and me.

We looked at each other like we'd made it past something big—something we couldn't see over the top of before. And we got there by boosting each other up and climbing on top of each other's shoulders.

Andre made Miss Della stop class for a minute.

"Part of the family solved a math problem back here that nobody could do before, even me," Andre announced. "Ivy pushed us to do it, and Mario was the first one to get it right. Now when the rest of you go to take your GEDs, we can teach you, too. That's why we're a family—the members that are further along pull the other ones up to the next level."

"Congratulations to all of you! Ivy, Tony—I mean Mario," said Miss Della, catching herself as she clapped.

All that week the dog was quiet. His gate was closed most of the time, and he didn't charge the fence once. But his eyes followed me close every time I walked past.

Spiers called that weekend and told my mom the DA didn't need me to testify yet. That my statement would be good enough for the grand jury. But that when Watisick came to trial, the DA would put me on the stand for sure.

"I'm personally going to coach you, Clay," Spiers said, after Mom put me on the phone with him. "Watisick's lawyers are going to be slick. They'll try to change your story around and make you say things that didn't happen. You don't want to be their puppet up there. I'll show you how to stand your ground and keep them off you."

I didn't say a word back to him.

"I know this is difficult for you, Clay. But your family and the community needs you to be strong, and clear—very clear—on what happened that night," said Spiers, hanging up the phone.

My dad told me that Spiers was just worried I'd get played for a sucker on the witness stand.

"It's like I told you, son—there are wolves in sheep's clothes everywhere," Dad said. "They act like they're your best friend. Then you see them for what they really are. I wouldn't be surprised if the lawyer they send to trip you up is black. That's how they play this game."

That night I dreamed I was in the courtroom, wearing the suit that Spiers bought for Addison. Watisick was standing in front of me, holding a stack of Bibles that reached up through the ceiling.

And the judge was screaming at me to put my right hand on the very top one and swear to tell the truth.

I woke up in the dark and heard the wind pushing hard against my bedroom window. So I pulled up the shade and looked out at the roof. Only it was dark there, too. And I figured that the wind probably put the candles out.

On Monday, Reggie was poking at Tony Soprano when he lost it.

"If I was gonna fight a girl, it would be you. You're half a man anyway," Tony snapped at her.

"Yeah, what half do you want to fuck with, the front or the back?" Reggie said.

After everything calmed down, Tony told Miss Della that he was tight because his father's deli got stuck up Saturday night.

"He's all right, I hope. All they got was money?" asked Miss Della.

"Yeah, nothin' happened to him," said Tony. "But these two niggers with guns came in and—"

"Wait! Wait!" Miss Della stopped him. "Who came in?"

"I told you, two niggers with guns," said Tony.

Latoya bounced down the hallway screaming, "Tony said 'nigger'! I heard him. He said 'nigger'!

He said two niggers robbed his daddy's store."

"I know you're upset, but why would you use that word to me?" Miss Della asked him, with everybody on Tony's shoulder.

"Why? They weren't black with a job, like you. These were niggers with guns," he answered.

"I told you he said it! I told you!" Latoya kept on.

"You see! That's why he don't eat with us!" said Reggie. "He thinks we're fuckin' animals!"

"That's bad business, Tony," said Bell. "You need to forget you know that word."

"Why?" Tony asked him. "You and everybody else here uses it all the time—my nigga this, my nigga that. He's my nigga, she's my nigga—yo, nigga."

"Stop!" said Miss Della. "I never used that word here, and neither has Andre. So don't say everybody!"

"But *they* all do," Tony said, pointing at the other kids.

"We don't mean it the same way you do," said Ivy.

"You're not black, so you can't say it without gettin' stomped," Reggie told him.

"*He* says it every day," Tony said, looking right at Cruz.

"Yeah, but I'm not white," said Cruz.

"But you're not black," said Tony, really getting hot.

"Oh my God. He doesn't get it!" Reggie said. "But *he's* not white. *You* are!"

I wanted to bang my head against the wall just to get that shit out of my ears. Then I closed my eyes, and everything was black. But that didn't make it any better, so I turned my back on all of them, walking away from that whole mess.

"From now on, nobody's allowed to say that word here!" said Miss Della. "I don't care if you're black, purple, or green. I don't want to hear it!"

It didn't end there. Reggie dropped a slip into the complaint box on Tony for what he'd said. Andre handled it right before we left. He said that because Tony was talking garbage, he should clean up outside of Daytop to get himself straight with the family. Tony didn't argue a lick. He was walking to the closet for the broom and dustpan before Andre had even finished.

We were headed out the door, and Tony was still sweeping outside with Andre watching.

"Don't forget about that pile of dog shit," Latoya said, laughing.

"That's right," said Reggie. "That's garbage, too."

"I don't even pick up my own dogs' shit," Tony said.

"That's part of the job," said Andre, handing Tony a plastic bag.

"Oh, I got to see this," said Reggie. "Come on, clean it up!"

That's when the dog started barking from behind his gate.

"See! That dog wants you to be his maid," Bell said.

Tony's face turned blood-red. Then he broke the broom in two and slammed the pieces down in the street with the dustpan.

"Fuck you all!" said Tony, walking away. "Fuck every last one of you! I'm nobody's maid. Take the fuckin' broom and shove it up your ass, all of you!"

Andre stayed calm, and called after Tony, "Don't come back unless you bring your father with you."

Reggie and Latoya were laughing, and Cruz said something nasty in Spanish.

"Some of you really need to grow up," Ivy said, heading in the other direction.

"That's the smartest thing I've heard so far today," said Andre.

Then Andre said that one of the family members needed to finish the job. And since Reggie was the one who dropped the slip, Andre handed her the plastic bag.

"You thought it was important enough to call him out on, and I agreed," Andre told Reggie. "He falls down, so you pick up for him—family style."

"He's no relation of mine anymore," said Reggie, bending down for the shit.

Reggie tied the bag up tight, holding it out away from her nose. And when she let it go, I heard it hit the bottom of the garbage can.

If Andre had asked me to finish for Tony, I don't know what I would have done just because it was that monster's shit. But if I did pick it up, I wouldn't have dropped it into that can. I'd heard enough by then and probably would have waited for that dog to run at the fence, and smashed his own shit in his face.

On the way home, I saw a little kid blowing soap bubbles with his father. They were sitting on the same bench where Addison and me saw those two women. So I crossed over into Rainey Park and walked past them slow. I listened to them laughing together and watched the light shining through all the bubbles. And one of them landed on my shoulder before it popped.

I walked down the hill to the East River. The smokestacks from the power plant were puffing white smoke into the sky. I remembered how a news story I read during morning meeting said that the smoke coming out of them was really black. But the power company added a chemical to turn it white. Then people wouldn't complain about it, and think it was part of the clouds.

I stared out at the water and watched the tide pull everything in one direction. Then I circled back up past the baseball field where that hardball smacked me in the mouth when I was a kid. I thought about Addison telling me that baseball players couldn't cry with all the people watching from the stands. But the park was almost empty. And if I could cry, the tears would have come out of me till they rolled down the hill and flooded that river.

I turned around and looked back at the smokestacks. Only they didn't remind me of giant blunts anymore.

When my dad got home that night, he said

there were cops all over the next corner. That they had five or six people in handcuffs and were loading them into a black van.

"I saw Darrel watching from down the block and asked him if it was a drug sweep. He wasn't sure, or didn't want to say in front of his friends," Dad said. "God, I hope he's got the good sense to keep clear of all that shit on the street."

CHAPTER 11

RIGHT BEFORE THE start of morning meeting, Andre said that Angel had something special to share. I thought it was going to be a drawing, but it wasn't.

"Before he left us, Addison Reynolds said he'd memorize the philosophy, and recite it alone one morning," said Andre. "It was difficult for Addison because he struggled with his reading and had a learning disability. It was a goal he set for himself and never got a chance to reach. The philosophy's been hard for Angel, too, because of his English. But he wants to pick up for a family member, so Angel's gonna recite it for us now."

"This for Addison," said Angel, looking right at me.

Everybody stood in a circle with their hands on each other's shoulders. And something shot through me that lifted me up onto the tips of my toes.

"I here because I can no longer hide—from who—I am," Angel started off.

But after that, I wasn't listening to the words anymore. I was tuned in to the sound of Angel's voice, and thinking how I needed to finish something for Addison, too. That I had to make Darrel quit the corner, no matter what.

"Fearin' not the soul-tude of death, but re-joice in my love for others," ended Angel.

Then there was nothing but the sound of hands clapping and my heart pounding inside my chest.

All that day, I kept looking over at Angel's picture of that kid who looked like Addison on the corner between the light and dark. And every time I looked, I saw Darrel's face on top of that kid's shoulders now.

At around six o'clock, I saw my dad pull up in his truck from our living-room window. He was always the last one to leave work, so I figured my uncle would be home already. I called, and he was in the middle of dinner. I told him it was about

Darrel. That it was important, and couldn't wait another day.

"Six thirty, sharp," he said. "I'll be outside your building."

I sat out front waiting for him, with the roll of bills inside a tight fist. I closed my eyes and listened to the cars roar past. They came fast, one after another, trying to beat the light on the corner. Sometimes they'd run up on top of each other, and I'd hear their brakes screech. And when the street went quiet, I knew they'd got caught behind the light. But inside of a minute, there'd be another round of cars ripping by. That's the way it is on 21st street—there's traffic 24/7.

I heard the heavy truck slow down, and my uncle pulled up next to where my dad parked. I climbed into the front seat, and before either one of us said a word, I opened my fist and held out the money.

"That's how Addison got to the roof that night. He was chasin' after this," I said, with my hand trembling.

"I don't even want to touch it," my uncle said, cutting off the engine.

Then I told him all about Darrel dealing crack on the corner, and how Addison didn't want him to be part of it. I kept talking, and heard myself telling the same parts of the story over and over again. And when I finally ran out of breath, I stopped.

"You did the right thing tellin' me all this, Clay," he said.

Then he asked me if Addison's mother knew about Darrel, and I told him no.

"I'll handle it from here," he told me. "You go back inside with your family."

But I wouldn't get out of the truck, and said I had to see it through to the end.

My uncle turned the key, and I felt the vibrations from the engine run up my spine. Then he took off the hand brake and turned the truck back around.

We double-parked on a side street and saw Darrel on the corner with two other guys. My uncle wrapped both hands around the steering wheel, putting his face up to the windshield to see better. A car pulled up to them, and Darrel was doing the talking. That's when my uncle shot across the intersection and pulled up right behind that car, honking his horn all the way. That car took off, running the red light.

The guys with Darrel almost split, too, thinking we were cops.

"You think the po-lice roll in a laundry truck?" Darrel screamed. "That's my part-time pops and fuckin' cousin!"

"This ain't no playtime, Pops," one of those guys said. "Get outta here 'fore you get yourself hurt!"

But Addison's father stepped to the guy, and hit him hard in the ribs. The guy dropped to the ground, gasping for air. Then the other dude helped him up, and they both ran.

"I see how your boys got your back," my uncle said.

"You want to see who I am?" Darrel screamed back, charging straight at him.

In the second it took for Darrel to reach him, I felt like I was back on that rooftop. I could see Addison jumping out in front of that door with his wallet. Only this time there weren't any shots, and the air didn't catch on fire.

My uncle grabbed Darrel by the shoulders, driving him into the side of the white truck. And I could see the metal give when Darrel's back slammed up against it.

"I already know who you are," his father said. "You're my son!"

With all his strength, Darrel tried to break loose, but he couldn't.

"Maybe I need to know you a lot better, but you're still my son," said his father. "And you're not gonna be some drug dealer on the street. I already lost one son that way!"

Then my uncle dug his hand deep into Darrel's front pocket, and pulled out a rock of crack.

"This is for sale, right?" asked his father.

But Darrel didn't answer, and turned his head away.

"Give him the money, Clay!" my uncle demanded.

I opened my hand and held the roll of bills in front of Darrel's face.

"Go on, take it! That's the exact same money your brother died over!" his father said. "Take it!"

"I don't want it!" Darrel screamed. "I don't want it!"

"Put it in his pocket!" my uncle told me.

And after I did, he turned Darrel loose. Then my

uncle stepped off the curb and threw that rock down the sewer.

Darrel was leaning up against the truck, crying.

I watched the tears coming down his cheeks. Then I felt for the hole in the middle of my chest, and knew for sure it was starting to close up.

"Now we're goin' upstairs to your mama's house. Together, we're gonna tell her what you been doin'," Darrel's father told him. "And I will never catch you out here again."

Darrel's eyes were on the roll in his front pocket.

"Do you understand me, son?" his father said, with the sound starting from deep inside his belly.

"Yeah, Pop," Darrel said, raising his head.

My uncle looked me dead-square in the eye. And we stayed locked together that way till he turned his head to climb into the truck with Darrel. Neither one of us had to say a word. I knew it was a look that only gets passed between family—a look that you can hold on to when you can't trust anybody else to watch your back.

Then the engine turned over, and I took a deep breath. There were long shadows running across the street. On the side of that truck, I saw the elephant with the soap bubbles coming out of its trunk pull away from the corner and into traffic.

Over the next few days, I didn't watch a second of TV or do anything else but study for the GED. I went over all five sections of the test from top to bottom. Even the parts I had down cold, I studied again just to make sure.

I had three textbooks spread out on my bed when my dad came in with an extra lamp. He screwed in a new bulb, and my bedroom was filled with light.

"That's better," Dad said. "I don't want you havin' to squint to see."

He grabbed a book off my bed and started reading to himself. He never graduated high school or got a GED. But I knew his math was strong from figuring out his business. So I showed him a percentage problem, and he nailed it right away.

When he was done, Dad looked at me and said, "Your uncle told me you were startin' to see things clear, and becomin' a man. I just want you to know that I'm proud of you and what you did for Darrel."

Then he leaned over before I could move and hugged me tight. And when I was wrapped up inside his arms that way, it felt like nothing in the world could make a dent in me.

Tony Soprano never brought his father back to Daytop. So the counselors cut him from the program and left him to deal with his PO on his own. But they were still letting him take the GED. Andre and Miss Della decided to let Bell stay until his PO could find him another program. They put him on contract, and made both Bell and his mother sign. It said that if his urine came up dirty one more time, he'd be discharged from the program the same day. And soon as Bell broke the news to kids, Reggie said out loud what the rest of us were thinking: "If they pack your ass upstate to residential, you can come home anytime you want. Just start walkin'."

The closer the DA got to picking a grand jury, the newspapers started having stories about the shooting again. There was even one about Addison's mother crying at her job. Spiers couldn't do anything for her, and blamed the mayor. But the day after that story hit, she got transferred over to taking calls from people who had complaints about their landlords.

Andre explained to kids that there were twenty-three people on a grand jury. That in Queens, more than half of them would be black and Spanish for sure. And that some of them might even live in a city housing project.

"The DA just needs to get a majority—that's twelve people—to say there's enough to look at to have a trial," explained Andre. "And that's gonna happen here, or the DA wouldn't have brought charges. There's a saying, and it's true—the DA could indict a ham sandwich if he wanted to. It's that easy. He comes on and says why he thinks you're guilty, and the other side doesn't get to poke holes in what he said. Usually the other side doesn't say anything at all. They save it for the trial."

One morning, I walked into Daytop and Darrel was sitting in Miss Della's office with his mother and father. Miss Della saw me in the hall and waved me inside. My aunt and uncle both got up to hug me, but Darrel stayed glued to his seat.

"Obviously, I don't need to make introductions. Soon as his paperwork's ready, Darrel is goin' to be joinin' us at Daytop, Clay," said Miss Della.

Then she asked Darrel if he was going to have

any beef with me over the way he got here.

"No, he isn't," his mother said for him. "Clay's family, and he helped save Darrel's life."

But Miss Della wanted to hear it from Darrel, and asked him again. It didn't matter to me. And I wouldn't have took back what I did for anything.

"I got no beef with my cuz," said Darrel, finally looking up at me. "It's just what happened. It's over."

I reached out a fist to him, and Darrel gave me a pound.

Then Miss Della called me a success because I'd stayed clean and was taking my GED in a couple of days.

"That's impressive, especially through this tragedy," Darrel's father said.

"It is," said Miss Della. "Clay's learned what it means to stand up for something. Not to let anybody else tell you what the truth is when you've seen it with your own eyes. I know Jackson Spiers has helped him to understand that."

But I could see my reflection in the window behind Miss Della. And I knew that wasn't me she was talking about.

CHAPTER 12

THE GRAND JURY hearing was just a few days off. And I saw a story on TV where a reporter asked Watisick's lawyer if his client was sorry for Addison getting killed.

"He's certainly remorseful over it," the lawyer said.

I almost went to the dictionary to look up the difference. But I had enough to think about with what came out of my own mouth.

That dog was behind the locked gate on my way to Daytop. He let out a whine and followed me along the fence. Then something growing inside of me made me stop. I turned to square off with him, and felt like the street was as much mine as his.

He stuck his nose through the fence and started

sniffing at me, like he wasn't sure who I was anymore.

I climbed the steps to Daytop, and Andre was at the front desk.

"It's a new time for all of us," he said. "Go on upstairs and see."

Darrel was in the kitchen eating breakfast. I could hear that kids already knew he was Addison's brother. They were asking him all kinds of questions, and I never saw a new kid get treated so nice. I guess it was out of respect for Addison and what Darrel was going through.

At morning meeting, after we said the philosophy and read the horoscopes and weather, Miss Della asked Darrel to introduce himself to the family.

"I'm Darrel Reynolds. I'm sixteen years old, and before I got here I was at Long Island City High School. My moms and pops made me come here 'cause I was sellin' drugs and smokin' weed."

One at a time, everybody told Darrel their name and how old they were. When it was my turn, I listened close to the sound of my voice, and thought it was different—maybe stronger. Then Miss Della asked the family to give Darrel a round of applause.

"Tell Darrel why we're clapping for him, Clay," said Miss Della.

"We're not clappin' 'cause you're here," I told my cousin. "We're clappin' 'cause you made it here, to a clean and sober environment."

And after the words came out of my mouth, I looked down at where my own feet were on the floor. I thought about how high I climbed to get here. But I still couldn't see over the top of my lie about Addison's wallet.

That day, Reggie and Bell were taking turns spinning the globe. They'd close their eyes and shove a finger down to stop it. Whatever place their finger landed on was where they belonged.

Reggie put her finger down in Mexico, and Bell split his sides laughing.

"They grow so much weed there you'll never stop smoking," he told Reggie.

"You spin, and I hope you get upstate New York, 'cause you belong in residential," she came back at him.

"Yo, I landed in Chad. That's right next to Nigger!" said Bell.

"That's Niger, asshole!" Reggie ranked on him.

"Why would they name a country 'Nigger'?"

That's when they both jumped on me to try.

"Come on, Clay. Let's see where you belong," said Bell, spinning the globe.

So I shut my eyes and stabbed a finger down.

I was in the middle of the Indian Ocean, beneath the equator. Then I gave it a second try, but when I opened my eyes, my finger was surrounded by blue again.

"Atlantic Ocean!" Reggie said. "Damn! Don't drown on us, Clay."

On my last go, I came down in the Pacific Ocean and just walked off.

"Look, Clay," Bell yelled after me. "You were on this tiny dot—Wake Island. You got a little pebble to stand on—to keep from sinkin'."

My last night of studying, I stayed up till almost two o'clock in the morning. I had my books out on the bed with my legs tucked up underneath me. I shut the light a couple of times, just to give my eyes some rest. And every time I did, I felt like I was on a raft out in the middle of the ocean. That there was nothing around me but darkness. Then I'd raise up my head and see the light on the rooftop through my window. Some part of me wanted to jump out of bed and run there. But I held on to myself tight from the inside and flipped the light switch on instead.

The GED test was at LIC. I showed my ID, and the guards gave me a pass to go upstairs. I started out with the hallways almost empty. Then the bell went off to change classes, and there was a flood of kids. Somebody going in the other direction called my name, but I couldn't see who it was.

I knew the room number where I was headed. It was on the far end of the building, and I remembered having a class there as a freshman.

First Addison went to LIC. Then me, and Darrel. The year before, for a little while, the three of us were there at the same time. Now everything was different.

When I got to the room, Ivy and Tony Soprano were both there already. They were sitting right next to each other, and I took the seat behind them.

"I'm in a better program now—a private one," Tony said, bouncing his eyes between Ivy and me. "One my father has to pay a lot for, with kids from my own neighborhood."

"How's the food there?" Ivy asked him, giving me a half-smile.

"It's good," Tony answered quick. "It's real good. I got no problem eatin' what they cook."

The test was supposed to start at ten o'clock. But it took us almost an hour to do all the paperwork first. And by the time I finished bubbling in every letter of my name with a number-two pencil, my arm was going numb.

For the writing part, I had to do a five-paragraph essay. Everybody in the room got the same question: *When people evaluate who they are, they often look back at a significant event in their life that influenced them. Discuss one event in your life and how it helped determine who you are today.*

If there was a mirror in front of me, I probably would have stared into it till the test was over and not written a word. But I looked down at the paper and started filling up the blank spaces between the blue lines fast.

I couldn't write about the rooftop. So I picked the morning I met up with Addison again at Daytop, and what that meant to me.

Addison put his arms around me and we were a

family again. He heard about my problems and I heard about his. I watched how he handled himself and that made me feel stronger inside. Before he died, Addison trusted me with things he wouldn't tell anybody else. We started out being cousins that first morning, but before he died we got to be like brothers, I ended it.

I knew I'd skipped around all the bad parts. But it had enough of the truth that it didn't bother me when I put my pencil down.

I finished the grammar questions that counted with the essay. Then we did the science and social studies parts after that. The teacher put the time up on the board every ten minutes. I kept up a good pace and had enough time to go back over the hardest questions.

There were lots of adults taking the test, too. I could see some of them were having a tough time. And I wondered how they felt taking a test with kids and struggling like that.

They gave us a twenty-minute break and let everybody go outside for some air. People were fiending for cigarettes. One of the adults even went across the street and took a hit of weed. I was beat from all the questions and just wanted to breathe.

A different teacher gave us the second part of the test. He kept looking over at where we were sitting. At first, I figured he thought we were cheating off each other. But he was trying to scope out Ivy. His wedding ring didn't hold him back one bit. And if we were out on the street, the drool probably would have been hanging over the side of his mouth.

The literature part was the easiest for me. But I still had to read a bunch of stories and poems, and concentrate on every one of them. When I got to the math section, I kept waiting for the question with the circles to come up. And every time I turned the page in the booklet, my eyes went sideways trying to find it. I thought maybe I'd get away easy. That it wasn't even on my test. Then I saw it on the next-to-last page.

The two circles were exactly the same as the problem I'd been studying at home. So I already knew what the right answer was, and wrote it in. When I finished with the rest of the math, I went back and did the circle problem anyway. Step by step, I watched the answer come out the way I knew it had to.

Ivy was already handing her test in.

"Ivy—what a lovely name," said the teacher, reading it off the top of her paper.

But Ivy never blinked at that bastard, and I wanted to get up and smack him bad.

Tony Soprano had a different-colored test than mine, with different questions. And I could see him figuring out his circle problem over and over.

It was a little after five thirty, with just a few minutes left in the test. But I didn't give my paper in right away. I just sat there exhausted. The GED takes six weeks to grade. It gets sent upstate to Albany, then they mail you the scores. But that wait was going to be easy. It's what was coming tomorrow that had me tight, when the DA would go after Watisick.

For a long time that night, I looked at Watisick's picture in the newspaper. I tried to see past his eyes, but I couldn't.

I wouldn't see Watisick tomorrow; neither would Addison's mother or father. The grand jury hearing was closed off to everyone except for Watisick, his lawyers, the DA, and anybody they called to testify. The press wasn't even allowed inside.

"We're prepared for something to happen," said Watisick's lawyer in the story. "A large percentage of the grand jury is African-American. And considering how the police commissioner tainted this process, these jurors will be under tremendous pressure from their communities to move forward with an indictment."

Even with Addison pointing his wallet at them, maybe those cops still should have held back. Maybe they should have yelled "Police!" so Addison would have known who it was.

I didn't feel like I was sticking it to Watisick anymore, or protecting Addison. At first, Spiers had me sold that I was standing up for everybody in the projects, and could stop black and Spanish people from becoming target practice. But things had finally come into focus for me, and I didn't buy that anymore, especially from him.

Lying about the wallet was really about me being afraid to say what I knew.

I finally fell asleep that night with what really happened stuck inside my throat. The words wouldn't come out, but I couldn't swallow them back down again either.

That next morning, I got dressed and left for

Daytop without having to say a word to my mom or
dad. I walked past Clorox's building and looked up
at the roof. Only I had to raise my hand to block out
the sun, and I couldn't see it clear. I passed on the
other side of the street from Rainey Park, and all
three smokestacks from the power plant were
going full blast.

I turned the corner to Daytop, and that dog's
gate was swung wide open. But I wasn't shook over
it. I pulled everything up inside of me, and kept on
going.

He was sitting in front of his house, looking
right at me. And I wouldn't take my eyes off him. I
thought about how much Addison lost, and all the
pain our families felt. Then I thought about everything I'd been through. I didn't care anymore that
the gate was open. I stopped before the end of the
fence and grilled that dog like I was better than he
was. That nothing he could do would ever hold me
back again.

I heard him growl and run to the gate. But I was
already headed towards Daytop, and I wouldn't
even turn back around to look at him.

Inside, the front desk was empty. Andre was in

his office, talking with a new kid and his parents. He came into the hall to say something. That's when he looked down at my feet and the floor behind me. I'd tracked dog shit through half the hallway.

"I was going to introduce you to our new family member, but that can wait," Andre said, shaking his head. "Go back outside and clean off your shoes. Then I need you to mop up this floor with bleach."

I was angry as anything for stepping in that bastard's shit. I went back outside, knowing he was still out there. The same way I knew I had to tell the truth about Addison and the wallet. My eyes were finally open all the way. I was standing in the light, at the very top of something. And I'd made up my mind: I wasn't going back down into the shadows.

HE RAISED HIS head and tail at the same time and started towards me. I could hear his nails scraping the sidewalk over the sound of my breathing. A Mack truck ripped around the corner. The roar from its engine kept building inside my ears, till a wall of air rushed up against me. But I didn't pull back an inch and stepped straight through it as the steel grill flew past my face.

We were maybe ten feet apart when my knees locked tight. His eyes got small and sharp. I felt the muscles in my arm shaking. I tried with all my might to hold them still, and when I finally did, the lid over my right eye started to twitch. There was a growl that began in his belly and rumbled through his throat. I tried to stare him straight in the eye. But he let out a short bark that sent a shock wave through me. Then he tore his teeth through the air, shaking his head from side to side. And I felt like I was already clamped between his jaws.

He shot forward in one leap. I caught him inside my chest, and he knocked me back a step. I tried to shove him off, but I couldn't. And I'd never had my arms around anything so strong and vicious before. His teeth were in my face, and every muscle in my neck was straining to pull back. I stared down the black-and-brown roof of his mouth. He was up on his hind legs, almost walking, and every bit of strength I had was pushing against him.

My thumb got hooked inside the corner on his jaw, and I shoved my other hand up into his grill to get it loose. His teeth cut across the tops of my knuckles. The growls never stopped, and inside of them were sounds I didn't know existed. His skull slammed sideways into mine, and for a second I saw stars. My left knee buckled and cracked against the cement. In a heartbeat, I was flat on my back with both hands jammed up against his throat. Then I kicked my foot up hard between his legs, and heard him cry.

I was scared to death, but I was fighting back.

And something deep inside that he couldn't get to wouldn't let me quit.

I felt his teeth sink into my side, and the warm blood soak through my clothes. He dropped his weight back, lowering his head almost to the ground. Then he twisted his neck and tried to shake me in his mouth. I punched at his ribs till I finally heard a gulp of air pop out of his throat. He let me loose, and there was maybe a foot between us.

The guy from the tire shop ran at us, screaming for the dog to stop. He was swinging something metal, and the dog backed off before the guy ever got close.

I don't know how, but I got up to my feet. Everything was spinning. I saw the guy's gray overalls jump in front of me, and for a second, I thought that bastard dog was coming back for more. I didn't want the guy touching me, but he kept trying to hold me still. Then I saw the steps to Daytop and shoved him off. I lifted my leg for the first step and felt the air flowing through my lungs. I reached out my arm and grabbed for the doorknob. I squeezed it inside my scraped-up palm, and the sting shot up my arm.

I was drifting in and out, and I heard my mom's voice, calling soft, "Clay. Clay." Then my eyes focused all at once, and I saw the light in the window from my bed.

Mom was holding my hand, running her fingers over the scratches on my cheek. Dad was on the other side of me in his white laundry uniform, with a tight grip on my wrist.

The doctors at the emergency room didn't stitch up my side. They said that dogs have plenty of germs, and if the bite got infected, they'd only have to rip everything out again. So they patched me up with tape and said that sooner or later it would heal on its own. Then they gave me some pills for the pain and sent me home.

My mom was cursing that dog, saying he should be put to sleep.

"It's how that damn dog got raised up," Dad said. "That's the problem. There's always gonna be animals like that."

But I looked at them both like they didn't have to worry about me. That after this, nothing could ever touch me again. I'd proved I didn't have to take shit from anybody. Not that dog, not Spiers—no one.

Then they stopped to hear the TV over by the window. The news bulletin said the grand jury didn't indict Watisick. That his lawyer had him testify, and when he talked about shooting Addison, he broke down crying.

The DA said the grand jury believed it was an accident, and not a crime.

Spiers came on and called the DA a puppet for the mayor. "It's all in how it gets presented," said Spiers. "A DA can lead a grand jury anywhere he wants it to go. My sources tell me the DA gave them as little as possible to work with, praying they wouldn't make the leap for themselves. But I can assure you that the Reynolds family will be filing federal civil-rights charges against all three police officers."

For all the system knew, Addison was trying to show those cops his ID. But Addison was a black kid on the roof of one of the Ravenswood Houses, and that gave the cops some kind of right to be nervous and have their guns out. And for some reason of politics, the DA found a way to tell that story to a grand jury of mostly black people so they'd vote that it wasn't even close enough to being a crime to have a trial over.

I curled up in my mom's arms with all that running through my brain, and finally cried. That hole inside me had closed. I'd got strong enough to grieve for Addison right and move ahead with my life.

I cried, and I couldn't stop.

Turn the page to read an excerpt

from Paul Volponi's next book:

Rucker Park Setup

Prologue

A FATHER SHOULDN'T have to outlive his own son. It's not right.

My pops died when I was too little to remember. And without the pictures my mom kept, I wouldn't even know what he looked like.

Stove was like my second pops, and he did things with me I never got a chance to do with my real flesh and blood. His son, J.R., was my best friend since fifth grade and lived in the same apartment building as me. It didn't matter that I'm black and they're Puerto Rican. We got to be almost family. But I don't deserve any more best friends. Not after the way I played J.R., and ran off when he needed me the most.

I'd heard the sirens screaming up Frederick Douglass Boulevard, so I figured it was safe to get my chicken-ass back to the park. I watched from across the street and wouldn't get any closer. J.R. was lying on the basketball court under a green sheet, and his blood was on the ground all around him. Everything I'd done was weighing down on me, till moving my feet was like lifting two solid blocks of cement.

People were looking at me because they knew how tight we were. I didn't want to see inside anymore, and tried to keep my eyes on the high fence around Rucker Park. Then I saw Stove coming up the block in his mailman's suit, pushing a cart full of letters.

"That's the boy's father," somebody whispered, and the blood pumping inside me turned ice-cold.

I heard a voice beg Stove not to look. I shut my eyes tight but couldn't stop from opening them again.

An old lady came out of the crowd and threw her arms around Stove. He was down on one knee, crying in the street.

My best friend had just got stabbed to death right in front of me, and I didn't lift a finger to help him. I was too scared, and I knew that I still had to worry about my own skin.

I saw my reflection in a car window and wanted to spit on it.

I remembered Stove telling J.R. about the day he

was born. How he put his hand on J.R.'s chest to feel his heart beating. Only now my ears were stuck on the sound of kids bouncing basketballs. They were pounding the sidewalk, over and over, like heartbeats gone wild.

J.R. AND ME grew up the same—dreaming about winning the big basketball tournament at Rucker Park. We wanted it so bad that it got to be in our blood. We played on that court all the time, except those nights in August, when we'd just watch with our mouths hanging open. That's when the best pickup teams in the city would throw down in the middle of Harlem, right around the block from where we lived.

We could see it perfect from J.R.'s window. But we always wanted to be inside the park so we could feel it, too. Rucker Park is where some of the greatest pro ballers ever, like Dr. J and Wilt Chamberlain, squared off against street legends—guys with tags like Goat and Helicopter. Stove reffed lots of those famous games, before either J.R. or me was born. He's the head ref at the tournament now and always works the championship game.

J.R.'s pops had reffed our games since we were eleven years old, playing youth league. He never cut us a single break. Any call that was close went against us. I guess Stove wanted to teach J.R. and me to stand on our own, and show people he blew an honest whistle.

J.R. used to complain to his mother about it all the time, before she died from cancer a few years back.

"I thought blood was supposed to be thicker than water," he'd say to her, knowing his pops was listening in.

Then Stove would rip back, "There's only sweat on a basketball court, Mami. And it's salty, just like a baby's tears."

I was at J.R.'s crib the night Stove called from the hospital to say she'd passed away. We looked at pictures from her last birthday party, and J.R. couldn't stop crying. I left when Stove got home. But the second I walked out the door, I broke down, too. I sat on the stairs between floors in our building, bawling my eyes out.

That's when J.R. and his pops started to get even closer. And maybe I was a little jealous, because I couldn't stand even being in the same house with my mom's new husband and his big mouth.

The tournament here last summer was our first as players. We were going into our junior year then and were already starters on the squad at George Washington High School. But we mostly rode the bench behind older dudes with bigger bodies on a tournament team at Rucker Park.

Since then, J.R. shot up two more inches, to six-three. I was almost as tall, and we both hit the weights hard. We took George Washington deep into the play-offs this year, losing the semifinal game at Madison Square Garden. We were starstruck just to be standing on that court, looking up at all those seats. And we left the locker room there feeling like pros already.

J.R. got named All-City in the *Daily News*, and I got Honorable Mention. That's when the colleges started sending us letters our phones started ringing off the hook. Stove sat us down with an SAT prep book every night, and that gave me a good excuse to keep out of my house.

But Stove watched out for who came around, too.

"Street agents are fishin' for a piece of every kid with a future on the court. Snakes with cars and money will want to be your best friend. They front for management companies that can't contact a kid till he's done playin' in college and ready to turn pro," Stove warned us all the time. "They get their hooks into as many kids as they can. It's like buying up a hundred lottery tickets, and hopin' one hits big. I've seen them turn a poor kid's head with a new pair of sneakers."

That's why J.R.'s pops wouldn't let us play for Fat Anthony. He coaches Non-Fiction—a street team that's won the Rucker Park Tournament four times. Stove grew up with Anthony and knows his bag of tricks inside out. Everybody at the park knows Fat Anthony delivers kids to certain agents. That he bets on the games, and sometimes his players get a taste of that money.

"If college coaches hear you're mixed up in gambling, they'll give that scholarship to somebody else," said Stove. "It's not a game to Anthony. And son, I don't want you or Mackey mixed up in any of his dirty business."

I'd heard a new team called the Greenbacks was going after the best high-school talent around. J-Greene, a big-time rapper, started it up for the publicity and named the squad after his new CD, *In It for the Greenbacks*.

Greene showed up at Rucker Park with a fly shorty on each arm, and Tommy Mitchell, who used to play pro ball for the New York Knicks. Mitchell was coaching the Greenbacks. He already knew about J.R. and me, and wanted us both on the squad.

I didn't even have to think about it, but J.R. did.

"I definitely want to be down," J.R. told them. "But I gotta run it by my pops first."

Greene shot us a look like we were little kids. Then he turned to Mitchell and said, "I thought we was recruitin' men to wear my name."

"Trust me on this, G," said Mitchell, "these two got man-style game."

"Bless them!" barked Greene, snapping his fingers.

That's when his shorties gave us each a jersey the color of money, and a long kiss on the cheek.

"I get what I want," said Greene. "And when the honeys see you in those, and we win Rucker Park, you'll be gettin' plenty, too."

J.R. spent that whole night trying to convince his pops to let him join. I played him one of Greene's raps, but Stove hated it. He said it made Harlem sound like a war zone. After that, we kept hitting on how much we could learn from Tommy Mitchell, till J.R.'s pops finally caved and said it was all right.

We had a squad full of high-school all-stars, and a couple of ex-college players with muscle to back us up. And after our first practice together, J.R. and me knew the Greenbacks were going to be the bomb.

In our first tournament game, we were winning by almost forty points. The other team had a crew of older cats who couldn't keep up. But then we started rubbing it in, acting like real hot dogs. Mitchell got pissed over that and benched some of our guys.

Stove reffed that one and didn't stop the clock once inside the last five minutes. He was trying to get that spanking over with fast, before that other team figured they had to fight us to keep from looking like assholes.

Acorn announces the games at Rucker Park. He owns the barbershop down the block, and everybody knows him. He's big and thick, with a voice like Barry White from my mom's old records.

During the games, Acorn sits by the side of the court with a microphone in his hand. He's always got something quick to say. If you make a bonehead play, Acorn will dis you good in front of everybody. But when you do something right, he'll give you props for it, too.

If you're really special, Acorn gives you a nickname. And if the crowd hoots and hollers enough at that tag, it'll stick. It was Acorn who blessed some of the greatest street ballers with the tags that everybody knows them by.

The last few minutes of that first game was like a personal highlight tape of my best plays ever. It started with a pass I made through some dude's legs right to J.R. for an easy basket. The next time down court, I fired the ball off the backboard, and it looked like I was passing it to myself. Three guys from the other team came charging at me. But instead of catching the ball, I slapped it to J.R. for an open layup, and everybody watching roared.

"Hold the mustard on that hot dog!" Acorn echoed through Rucker Park.

Every time I touched the ball after that, Acorn called me "Hold the Mustard."

The crowd was loving it, too, till Mitchell yanked me from the game for showboating. But when I got to the sideline, Greene threw both arms around me, and Mitchell backed off. When the game ended, Greene brought the whole squad with him out to center court and rapped his big hit, "Up Yours."

That night, I went home with J.R. and his pops. There was leftover stew for supper, and a whole loaf of bread we finished off with the brown gravy. The walls held on to every bit of heat from that day, so Stove opened the windows wide, hoping for a breeze.

All J.R. and me could talk about was winning the championship, and how maybe Non-Fiction was the only crew that could keep us from it.

"You want something so bad, for so long. Then it's right in front of you," said J.R. over the TV and noise from the street. "You gotta check yourself to make sure it's really happenin'. And you gotta watch out, so you don't screw up and give it away, especially to that bastard Fat Anthony."

"But it's sweet!" I told him.

"Sweeter for you with that new tag," said J.R., dribbling a pretend ball between his legs, till we both cracked up laughing.

Then J.R. went to his bedroom window to find the star his mother taught him to wish on. She said it was the same star from the Puerto Rican flag and that it would always watch over him. But I didn't believe in that kind of stuff and stayed in the kitchen with Stove.

"You need *confianza*— faith in things, Mackey," said Stove. "Or else you better believe in yourself more than anything."

Those were just words to me then, with nothing behind them. But over the last few weeks they've been roaring in my head.

Now the championship game's in front of *me*. Rucker Park's packed tonight to see the Greenbacks finally take on Non-Fiction. But I'm not sure how much I believe in myself anymore, or what's really inside of me.

Stove's got the game ball under his arm and a whistle hanging from his neck. Only J.R.'s not here—because I fucked up so bad. And his killer's standing right there, cool as anything, like he doesn't have to think twice about me giving him up.